IF THE RING FITS

A WIT AND WHIMSY ROMANCE

SALLY JOHNSON

Copyright © 2023 Sally Johnson

All rights reserved.
No part of this book may be reproduced or transmitted in any form or by any means, electronic or mechanical, including photocopying, recording, or by any information storage and retrieval system, without permission in writing from the publisher, except for the use of brief quotations in a book review.

This is a work of fiction. Names, places, characters and incidents are either the product of the author's imagination or are used fictitiously, and any resemblance to any actual persons, living or dead, organizations, events or locales is entirely coincidental.

Cover design © 2023 LJP Creative

Published by Pink Bloom Publishing

Las Vegas, Nevada

First Edition 2023

❦ Created with Vellum

PROLOGUE

The path was lined with red rose petals. I squinted into the sunlight, following the line the petals created for me to follow. I wished I had my sunglasses, but wasn't allowed. The midmorning sun reflected off the water and straight into my pupils, basically blinding me, possibly permanently.

I could barely breathe. Not because of excitement for my anticipated proposal, but because I was squeezed into an evening gown. I looked down, even though I was supposed to look up, because I didn't want to step on my dress. The last thing I wanted to do was get tangled up, and fall on the uneven flagstone pavers and split a seam. They were randomly spaced, but placed there to look like they were a naturally occurring part of the landscape. I just knew I was going to stumble.

"Cut!" Al, the director, called. He was a larger man, and even in a muscle shirt (despite no muscles) and shorts, he was a sweaty mess. Moisture beaded up along his receding hairline and ran down his temples. It was warm, but the humidity heavy in the tropical air made it hotter than a sauna.

"Sweetie," said Al, "we need you to look up. You're walking to your future. The man you've fallen in love with is about to propose. Be proud. Be confident. Relax and smile."

Easy for him to say. How could I manage all those directions at once? I was supposed to be confident walking on uneven ground, smile while the sun was boring a hole in my cornea, and be relaxed? Sweat ran down my back in between my shoulder blades. What if it shorted out my mic? What if my excessive sweat caused pit stains, or even worse, butt-sweat stains?

In five minutes, Joshua, the beautiful man with the sexy smile and the killer dimples, would propose to me after six weeks of dating and in front of the whole country on the reality dating TV show *Desperately Seeking Mrs. Right*.

That was a lot to juggle in six-inch heels that pinched my pinkie toe.

Determined to get it right and *get there*, to hurry this process along because I really wanted to be engaged, I forged ahead. I was ready to be through with the "journey", off the reality dating show and on to happily ever after with Joshua. So, I did as I was told and made it to the proposal site without any more direction or interference from the film crew.

"Cut!" Al called out, holding up a hand to signal me to stop. The girl assigned to walk with me put her left arm in front of me and gripped her clipboard with her right hand.

"Hold on," she said in a low voice and then a heavy sigh. The humid filming conditions seemed to be taking its toll on everyone. Her bangs stuck to her forehead, and even when she blew up, trying to get her hair off her skin, it didn't work. How long had she been out here? It gave me hope that was the second filming of the day and not the first. If I was the first, chances were Joshua wouldn't be proposing to me.

A different girl carried a large white umbrella to shade me while the crew figured out lighting angles. This whole stop-and-start filming could make a five-minute proposal drag out to five hours. I considered slipping my shoes off and giving my toes a wiggle to make sure they were still alive. But I knew the moment I slipped one shoe off would be the exact moment they'd start filming again and then I'd have to scramble to get my shoe back on. And since there was sand everywhere, I'd probably end up with some in my shoe. That was the last thing I needed.

While the film crew shifted positions, I checked out the surroundings. The proposal site, although beautiful, was obviously not a naturally-occurring spot in Belize the show happened upon. We were at the edge of the waterfront, but there was about a five-foot rocky decline to the shore below. A spray would shoot up when the waves hit against the rocks, covering me with a fine mist of salt water. It might've been *refreshing* in any other situation. Right now, it only served as a distraction.

Oh. My. Gosh! My feet were killing me! I didn't have a watch on, but it had to have been at least twenty minutes since they paused filming. And I was still standing in my heels, my arches hating me and I was pretty sure I only had nine toes now. My pinkie toe had, for sure, curled up and died due to lack of circulation. At this point, I just wanted to get this stupid proposal over with. How much longer would we have to—

"Look alive everyone!" Al called out, and settled in his canvas director's chair. "Action!"

I rounded a corner to see Joshua standing there. A tent had been erected, wispy indigenous grass tufts clumped together in natural wood planters around the edges and flowers climbed up the poles supporting the tent. If you looked closely, you could see the seams of the artificial stems. My artist's eye saw small gaps that I would've filled out more. But the overall appearance was one of effortless, natural beauty—an oasis of love.

The provided shade spared Joshua from the glare of the late-morning sun and heat and allowed him to look cool, calm and collected as he stood in a power stance, his hands clasped in front of him. His linen suit matched the feel of the tropical setting, and the only thing that gave away any sign of nervousness was the way he shifted his weight from one foot to another.

I stepped forward, thankful to be out of the sun. A headache tugged at the edge of my brain, thanks to all the squinting. I didn't want this, the best day of my life, to be ruined by a headache.

Joshua took two steps across the rug placed over the earth, flashed his dimples and hugged me. The hug reassured me and his familiar touch spoke to my soul. It'd be okay. It'd all work out. Our relationship had the potential to be amazing and if I could get out of this heat, I could appreciate the moment better. He stepped back and took both of my hands in his.

"Elsie, these last few weeks have been amazing."

Not the most original opening line for a proposal, but okay.

They *had* been amazing. But also so, so hard.

"And I never thought I would fall in love so hard or so fast."

My heart hammered against my chest in a staccato beat.

He smiled at me; a lock of his wavy hair fell onto his forehead. I wanted to reach out and brush it back into place.

"It's been a whirlwind, but falling in love *should* be a whirlwind."

He paused, which was my cue to share my feelings.

I had practiced my speech all morning. Thoughts about love, romance, and being swept off my feet was what I wanted to say. But at that moment, I couldn't form the words to adequately express how I felt.

Instead, I stood there, tongue-tied. I became keenly aware of a line of sweat trickling down my back.

A light breeze blew past my face—a gentle reminder to speak. "You're right," I said, finally finding some words. I felt like, in the situation, anything would be better than the excruciating silence. "Falling in love should be a whirlwind."

There was a one-second-too-long pause before Joshua picked up the cue to continue. He squeezed my hands in his and our eyes met.

Then he looked away.

"The thing is..."

What was happening? A weird feeling spread through me, almost like an adrenaline rush. He must've paused to gather his thoughts or find the right words. Maybe he forgot the proposal he had scripted out.

He swung our joined hands just a little, fidgeting. "I can't put into words how I feel about you exactly."

That sounded more like a proposal. He was back on track. I exhaled and closed my eyes.

"But it's not love."

My eyes popped open. "What?"

His eyes darted to the ground and his head drooped. "I love you, but I'm not *in* love with you."

I dropped his hands and stepped back. My heel caught on something, or maybe it was just the uneven sand beneath the rug that threw off my balance, and I stumbled. I caught myself, but still felt the heat from embarrassment spreading over my face.

"What?" I repeated.

His head bobbed up and down and then switched to shaking slowly side-to-side. "You're just not the right fit."

"I went to the Fairy Tale Suite with you. You promised!" My *whole family*, the whole TV audience, and the whole world knew I had spent the night with him. I *never* would've done something like that in such a public way if he hadn't promised to propose.

He shrugged. "Sorry."

Sorry? That was all he had to say? Did he think it was no big deal?

"I had to be sure I loved you in every way possible before I proposed," he said.

I literally saw red. I wanted to smash that square jaw with a right hook. Take out his straight nose with the heel of my palm. Claw out those beautiful, blue eyes with my perfectly manicured blush-colored nails. Pull out his hair in clumps, throw it in the wind in hopes the native birds could use it for their nests. And a knee to the—

"Elsie?"

I shook the fantasy from my thoughts, and looked at him, trying my hardest to keep my expression void of emotion.

"I'm sorry," he said while pulling me into an awkward hug. "I really tried. I wanted to love you. You are worthy of love—"

Worthy of love? Worthy of love? Did he think that I thought I wasn't worthy of love? That *wasn't* my problem! And not being worthy of *his* love? That was *not* something I was going to lose too many nights sleep over. What a jerk!

I inhaled deeply and exhaled, pushing down the impulse to lash out. I was supposed to be graceful and accept the news with poise. I had been given instructions by my handler/assistant/whatever-her-title-was while I got ready that I might not be proposed to. Or I might. Either way, the cameras kept rolling and I had to choose my actions accordingly. Easy for her to say when she was off-screen. I was in front of the cameras, in the glaring sun, the oppressing humidity, the heat of the day, with sweat trickling from every pore of my body, and I was supposed to be diplomatic?

I put my finger to his lips. "Joshua, Joshua, sshh," I said. "You're right. Everything you said is right." Emotions were bubbling closer and closer to the surface, threatening to overflow.

"I tried…" he started.

"Love should be a whirlwind," I said.

"It's not you, it's me…"

We were talking at the same time. I thought the director would've cut at that point, but maybe he wanted to let the scene play out and see where it went. But this was not a "scene" I would agree to do-over.

I kept on. "Again, you're right. You better believe that it's you and *not* me!" I kneed him in the groin and he went down, hands between his legs. I leaned down close to where he was on the ground. "And you should know, a whirlwind can take you down!"

I marched off the blanket. Instead of making the precarious walk to the limo in my heels, I pulled them off, threw them carelessly over my shoulder, and walked off set.

I might've been seeking Mr. Right, but I wasn't *that* desperate.

1

I skulked back into town just after midnight, pushing down a surge of guilt as I drove past the lighted-up, gilded, carved "*Welcome to Warren, Established 1747*" sign. I hadn't been home since the "hometown visits" for *Desperately Seeking Mrs. Right,* six months ago.

I slowed my car to a frustrating crawl as I rounded the corner coming off the bridge and navigated the small, two-lane street. *I miss the six-lane streets of Las Vegas.* The next driveway belonged to a utility building owned by the town. It was an old, red-brick building, covered with ivy: the perfect blind spot for the cops to hide and catch speeders.

Sure enough, a police SUV was parked exactly where I predicted. I smiled to myself. *Ha! Not catching me tonight!*

What I didn't predict was the vehicle's lights flicking on, glinting in my rear view mirror.

What the heck?

I glanced at my speedometer, confirming I was going the speed limit. I was *under* the speed limit. Surely, they weren't pulling me over for going too slow? I glanced at my mirror again. Maybe I just needed to let them pass. But they didn't.

I exhaled slowly, turned on my right blinker, and pulled into the closest convenience store parking lot. The lighted area made me feel safer at this time of night.

I do not need a ticket! I thought as I turned off the engine. Not only would I have to fork out the money, but my insurance rates would go up. Las Vegas was a crazy place to drive and the insurance rates reflected that. I racked my brain. Why was I stopped?

I rolled my window down and the cold, damp air rushed in, followed by the familiar scent of the salty sea. Warren was a seaside town in Rhode Island. The summers were humid and the winters were cold and wet. I preferred the mild winters of Vegas. Yet, here I was, back for Thanksgiving, freezing, getting pulled over for a stupid traffic stop. I hoped this wasn't a sign of how the rest of my visit would go.

I braced myself for the worst: a ticket. It couldn't be anything else. My registration was up to date, my car was definitely not stolen, and it hadn't been involved in any criminal activity (that I knew of).

As the officer stepped out of the vehicle, I could clearly tell from my rear view and side view mirrors that it was a man. Was that better or worse than having a female officer? Sometimes female officers were compassionate, but other times they were tough as nails. And it went the same for male officers. I wasn't below flirting with a cop, but the way I looked right now, in the final five minutes of my cross-country drive, was probably not very attractive.

A quick glance in the mirror confirmed my suspicions. My long, dark blonde hair hung lank, my gray eyes looked tired, make up hadn't touched my face in, at least, five days, and my heart-shaped lips could use some lip balm.

Did I smell? And if so, would he be able to smell it? I skipped the shower this morning at the cheap (and nasty) motel, opting to save time by getting on the road. Maybe I should've spent those extra twenty minutes showering, but was afraid I might pick up a staph infection.

I studied him as he approached, but my car mirrors could only help so much. Or so little. He had to be about my age, (even with the lights from the parking lot, it was still a little dim) tall, thin, probably brown hair.

At least it wasn't Officer Smitty, who was friends with my dad. He was a veteran cop in the town who was big and scary. If you got pulled over by him, there was no talking your way out of a citation. Even though I was twenty-nine, Officer Smitty was just as scary now as he'd been when I was a new driver at sixteen.

Realizing I should be prepared with my license and registration, I grabbed my phone and opened the wallet flap that held my license. I had just pulled it out when the officer reached my side.

"License and registration, please," he said, his voice bored, as if this was the tenth ticket issued this hour. He was definitely about my age.

I handed over the required documents. "Hi, yes, here." I shivered because of the cold air and it reflected in my voice.

Without saying a word, he walked back to his car. Was that a good sign or a bad sign?

I watched as he walked, noting he did look good in a uniform, at least what I could see from his waist down. The rest of his frame was covered up by his jacket. He got in the vehicle and shut the door. The weather being biting cold made me want to be ticketed and done. Home was less than five minutes away. Five minutes away after driving four and a half hours from New York City and this is where I get stopped by a cop.

I didn't know if it was best to stare straight ahead and

wait for him, or watch him, trying to have the most passive, innocent expression on my face. I decided on the second option.

When he reappeared at my window, I was able to get a better look at him. He looked like he belonged on a rookie cop show. All blue-eyed, straight nose and nice jaw. Kind of like a cute kid who grew up to be a cute guy. His youthful appearance was enhanced by his hair, which puffed up a little, but not in spikes, as if he tried to keep it down but it just naturally sprung up, doing what it wanted to do despite him.

He smiled, his teeth straight and even. He really had a nice smile. For a cop, I mean. I probably shouldn't have been checking out his smile while he had me pulled over. "Vegas, huh?" he asked. I noted the curiosity in his question and I relaxed a bit. If he wanted to chat me up, maybe he'd let me off with a warning.

I got that question all the time. People seemed to think it was just the Strip that existed and no one actually lived there.

"Yeah, Vegas," I said.

"Did you drive all the way from Nevada?" He pronounced it "Nev-aw-da."

I smiled because that was the test of a true native, how they pronounced our state. I was not in "Nev-add-da" anymore.

"I did. I'm here to visit my family. They just live on Company Street." I had also stopped along the way on my road trip to visit some old friends. And then hit traffic on I-95N because of a multi-car pile-up. And that's why I was here at 12:16 a.m.

He looked at my license again. "Just in time for Thanksgiving," he said.

"Gobble, gobble," I said. Oh, my gosh! Why did I say that? How embarrassing!

"Do you know why I pulled you over?"

I squinted in the poor lighting to see his name tag. "Listen, Officer McCutey—"

"Cutty," he said.

"Cutty," I repeated.

"It's Mick."

It sounded like he wanted to be on a first name basis. Or maybe a nickname. "Okay, Mick. I'm sorry. I wasn't trying to break any laws and I can't afford a ticket right now—"

"It's Officer McCutty," he said, slowly.

Was that so I'd finally get his name right? I was so tired I couldn't think straight. But I didn't want to admit that and have him think I was driving impaired. "Officer McCutty," I repeated.

"The reason I pulled you over," he looked at my license, again, "is because you have a tail light out."

I looked over my shoulder, even though I wouldn't be able to see the tail light. "Really?" I was perplexed. "I had that light fixed right before the trip. Weird. And that's not the only time it's been repaired."

He tapped my license on the rim of the window. "Either you have a short, or your mechanic has a crush on you."

Was he flirting with me? Surely the cop wasn't flirting with me. My shoulders relaxed a little as I considered his suggestion. "A crush?" I patronized a big chain repair shop, where I dealt with a front lobby man, usually never the same one, and not the person who worked on my car. The idea "my" mechanic had a crush on me was probably not the case. And from what I had seen at the shop when I'd been there, none of those employees were anyone I wanted to date.

"He wants you to keep coming back," he said and winked.

Okay, the wink was nudging me toward flirting. But he was a cop! Was that professional? Could he even do that?

"And here I thought it was just my car getting old."

He nodded. "It could be that, too."

Maybe not. Was I totally misreading everything?

"I'll have to see if Joe's Garage can check it out while I'm here," I said.

"Oh, yeah, Joe. I know him. I see him at the coffee shop in the mornings." The town was small enough that a coffee shop could be called *The* Coffee Shop and everyone knew where you meant. "So, you're visiting family? Are you in town long?"

I shrugged. "It's undecided. I'm at least here for Thanksgiving."

He handed me my license and registration. "Since you're going to be around…"

He paused.

Why? I waited. It almost sounded like he was going to…

He leaned in closer to my car, his hands resting on my open window. "You should get that light fixed. I'd hate to have to actually ticket you for that." His gloved hand offered me my license and registration back.

My chest deflated in relief. No ticket! Just a warning! Oh, good!

"Thank you, Officer McCutty! I owe you a coffee," I blurted out. "I really appreciate it."

Oh, wait. Did I just bribe a cop?

His expression remained neutral. "See you around."

I watched in my rearview mirror as he returned to his car. Wait. What? Did that mean he'd want a coffee or not? Was I going to see him around? Did I *want* to see him around? Based on his cute smile, I wouldn't *mind* seeing him around. As long as it wasn't in my rearview mirror.

I felt humiliated as I pulled back onto the street. Anyone driving by would know what was going on since the police lights were still flashing. I wished he'd shut off the tell-tale lights. But no, they kept flashing, announcing to the world my embarrassment.

I slowly and carefully navigated out of the parking lot and traveled down Water Street, making my way back home.

2

I crashed on the world's most uncomfortable Victorian sofa the night before, but woke to the smell of sausage and bacon. I was instantly in a better mood and my stomach grumbled in anticipation of breakfast.

I sent a quick text to my roommate that I'd made it home, then followed the *clink clank* of dishes in the kitchen to find a spread of scrambled eggs, bacon, sausage, toast and orange juice. I took some of everything. It all looked and smelled so good and suddenly I was *famished*.

"Good morning," I said as I joined the family in the dining room.

"Look who's up," Mom said.

The dining room table, with both leaves in, was a tight fit in the small room. My brother, Troy, his wife, Melissa, and their kids, Max (6) and Miley (10) filled one side of the table. Dad and Mom were at either end of the table, and my younger sister, Vivian (20), and Nana (79) sat down the other side of the table. I would have to squeeze by everyone to get to the only available chair at the far end, by the bay window.

Nana had been staying here and sleeping in my (former)

room. Ever since Gramps died a few years ago, having her live alone in her house and her general health and safety had been of increasing concern.

I bent down to give Nana a half hug. "How are you, Nana?"

"I'd be better if your dad would stop counting how many sausages I've eaten," she said. If Nana had a "spirit actress", it'd have to be Betty White. She had the white hair, the smiley personality and the pleasantly plump grandma body.

"Mom, you have to watch your blood pressure," Dad said.

"Oh, please, Charles! I'm going to die someday, in some way. If it's death by sausage, so be it!" With finality, she speared another link from her plate and took an exaggerated bite.

Things were a little spicy today, and it wasn't just the sausage.

I sucked in my breath and side-stepped past the china cabinet to the seat next to Dad. I prayed he wouldn't bring up anything about *Desperately Seeking Mrs. Right*, Joshua, or...the Fairy Tale Suite.

"Have you heard from that crum? What's his name? Joshua?" Dad asked.

He never failed to ask the hard questions.

"Nope. Haven't seen him, heard from him or thought about him." The last part wasn't true. I thought about him, sometimes, but not in a good way. More in a I-hope-his-life-is-miserable sort of way.

"How's your job?" Dad asked. If it wasn't hard questions, it was the same questions every visit. It was better to get them out of the way now than during Thanksgiving dinner this afternoon.

I chewed my bite of eggs good and thoroughly before I

swallowed. "Good. Business is good." I illustrated custom-ordered maps. It wasn't my business. I was subcontracted out to someone. My boss, Aaron, would send me the info of the map and I drew it. I liked it because it was flexible and I could work from anywhere.

"Do you regret not going to law school yet?" Dad asked. "Do you want to just draw maps your whole life?"

That was two really loaded questions that I wasn't in any rush to answer. Like I said, we had the conversation every visit because Dad didn't like that I chose art over college and went against his wishes. It'd been almost a decade and he still hadn't let go.

What I really regretted was that I wasn't accepted into Rhode Island School of Design. It was my first choice and a heavy blow when the rejection email came. It was another blow when Vivian was accepted two years ago.

"Work is going well, Dad." *That's all that matters*, I added to myself.

A cat darted across the lawn, leaving pawprints in the freshly fallen snow.

"Did you see that?" I said quickly, pointing to the window, hoping others saw it too. It was perfect timing, creating a distraction from the conversation at hand.

"Oh, yeah," Vivian said. "It's a stray cat that's been hanging around for a while."

"I've named him Cowboy," Nana announced. "Because he looks like a cow, and I think he's a boy."

"You can't tell from his—" Miley broke in.

"You're right honey, we can't," Mom said, then turned to me. "We see him most days."

Miley jumped out of her seat and ran to the window sill. "I wanna see the cat!" She dramatically looked both ways. Her brother followed suit.

"Waaaah!" Max moaned. "I didn't get to see the cat."

"No one's tried to save him?" I was a little alarmed. It was cold out there.

Vivian answered again. "He's afraid of us."

"Is that why he ran away?" Max asked in the same whiny voice, still craning his neck trying to catch a glimpse.

"Yes, honey, some cats live outside and don't have owners," Melissa explained.

"It probably belongs to the house down the street. The people moved," Mom said.

"And left their cat?" I was horrified. I looked around the table while everyone continued eating, seemingly not the least bit concerned about the cat outside. Shouldn't there be more cause for alarm?

Vivian shrugged. "That's when we started noticing him."

"They were horrible neighbors," my dad said, his voice gruff. "I wouldn't be surprised if they left the cat. They were horrible people. Horrible."

"What did they do that was so horrible?" I asked.

"They'd always park in front of our house. We should have that spot and they should know it." Dad used his fork, with a sausage attached, to motion to the exact spot outside that he was talking about.

The house next door was a rental house, and over the years a parking war had raged. It was a tired tangent of my dad's. That, along with the cat sighting, served as a great distraction from my lack-of-college-degree lecture that I'd gotten many times before.

I'd have to get that kitty a treat as a thank you.

"Now whose blood pressure is on the rise, Charles? You might want to reconsider eating that sausage," Nana said.

Oh, my gosh! I love her!

Nana deserved a treat too.

3

Who even likes sweet potatoes? Or yams? Or whatever they're called. Not me. And why do they have two names when they are the same thing? I gripped the steering wheel of my car. *Why was I sent out to get them?* Normally I wouldn't grumble, but nothing in this town was a quick trip, especially since there wasn't an actual grocery store *in* the town, only a small, neighborhood market. And, holy cow, it's Thanksgiving! I was pretty sure nothing was going to be open.

I cocked my head to one side, trying to crack the kink out of my neck from sleeping weird.

The kink stayed put. If I slept on the couch for too long, I'd have to get adjusted by a chiropractor. My body would be all sorts of out of alignment.

Being a holiday, the normal hustle and bustle on the narrow streets was missing. They were somewhat deserted in an eerie, *Walking Dead* sort of way. I could at least be thankful for that. After I turned onto Main Street, I saw a police car at Dunkin' Donuts and immediately thought of my tail light, which remained out of order. I hoped it wasn't

Officer McCutty and that whoever it was, they wouldn't take note of my car. All I really wanted at the moment was my sweet potatoes—actually my mom's sweet potatoes—and to not get pulled over again for the same thing. This time I probably wouldn't get off with a warning.

I slowly navigated the left onto Child Street and traveled well-within the 25-m.p.h. speed limit, even though I couldn't see the cop car in my rearview mirror. My careful right-turn into the store parking lot was rewarded with nothing. It was empty.

The market was closed.

Dang it! I pulled out my phone to check if they had holiday hours, but my phone was on red—five percent—to be exact, and died. I'd forgotten to charge it last night and meant to plug it in this morning.

I exhaled loudly, blowing my bangs out of my eyes and stared out my windshield at the entrance of the store, willing the automatic doors to part. Two minutes of watching for signs of life cemented the fact they were really closed. Great, now I had to go to a *real* grocery store, which also may or may not be open.

I needed caffeine. It was too early in the day to be dealing with this.

I couldn't go to Dunkin' Donuts, because the cops were there. Between the roofline, one street over, I could see the sign for Cumberland Farms, the closest convenience store. I could grab a Mountain Dew Code Red, get a little caffeine in my veins, and then continue my hunt for yams. Maybe I'd get lucky and the convenience store would have some. Who knew? It was a plan.

I left the convenience store with drink in hand, but without the yams. As I got in my car, I decided to go to Bristol. I took off, sipping the refreshing carbonation.

I looked left, intending to make a right turn on red. All was clear, so I proceeded onto the street.

The traction of my wheels skidded. *Did I just slip on some ice?* I was momentarily confused. It had been a long time since I'd driven on icy roads. I immediately took my foot off the gas to let the car slow down and righted my steering wheel. It was probably a puddle on the corner. I looked in my rearview mirror and saw one other vehicle approaching. Up ahead were traffic cones and a big orange sign announcing the right lane was closed. *Ridiculous.* Clearly no one was working on Thanksgiving. Had the road crew been too lazy to take down all the cones before the holiday?

I glanced in my rearview mirror, preparing to merge into the left-hand lane, then took a double-take.

The car behind me had caught up to me rather quickly, and was sliding *sideways* toward me. I jerked the wheel instinctively, hoping to move out of its path, but forgot about the traffic cones. I clipped them on my passenger's side, which slowed me down, but then I was thrown forward as the other car slammed into the back of me. I careened out of control, swiping the edge of another traffic sign, and spinning until I hit a telephone pole and slid into a ditch. My car came to a halt with an awful thud.

BAM! The airbag shot out and knocked my breath from me.

I was momentarily stunned. *Did that really just happen?* The silence didn't answer me.

What do I do next?

Should I get out of the car?

Should I stay in the car? I remembered hearing you should never move a body, I mean, person from a car in case they're injured—it might make the injury worse. Was I injured enough that I should stay put?

I looked at my lap. Blood was everywhere! The light red splatter was across my thighs, chest, hands. *Where was it coming from?* My heart felt panicky and I felt my blood pulse through my jugular. I was going to bleed to death!

I checked my forehead in the rearview mirror, but didn't see any open wounds. A welt had formed on my cheek and I realized it'd been from the impact when the airbag went off. I did a mental assessment of my body, carefully testing each part. My neck didn't seem any worse off than this morning. Ribs, collar bones, shoulders, wrists and elbows felt okay. Stomach felt fine, maybe a bit hungry since I was saving my appetite for the real feast this afternoon. No broken hips. My knees and legs felt okay. My feet and ankles felt fine. And no obvious bleeding.

When I unfastened the seatbelt, I searched for my purse. It was on the floor, the contents scattered in the puddle of Mountain Dew. *I just opened that!* The same red splatter that was on my hands was also on the inside door. I licked my skin and realized it was not blood, but Code Red. *I'm not bleeding to death. I'm going to live!* Relief flooded through me.

I took a couple of deep breaths as I gathered my thoughts and searched for my phone. I found it between the passenger seat and the door. The screen was cracked and sticky with soda, but it had been spared from the Code Red flood.

A knock at my window startled me and I sat up straight. A face was pressed against the glass. He looked like he belonged in Hollywood instead of Warren, Rhode Island.

"Are you okay?" he said loudly through the glass.

I nodded and held up my phone. "Just about to call 911."

"I already did," he said in the same loud voice.

Maybe he had, maybe he hadn't. I didn't know this guy and wasn't sure I wanted to take his word on that. He could be one of those weird serial killers who gets into accidents on purpose so he can kidnap and torture his victims. Okay, maybe I'd been watching too many reruns of *Criminal Minds*, but in my defense, I didn't think it was bad to take precautions.

I went ahead and made my own call to 911.

It was cold and I didn't want to stand in the freezing air, waiting for emergency personnel to respond. But I knew I should check the damage to my car and talk with the guy.

Be calm. Don't take the blame (because it wasn't my fault). *Take pictures. Get insurance info from him.* Thoughts ran through my head, but I couldn't prioritize them.

The other vehicle—a sleek, marigold-colored SUV—was parked up ahead of me. Most of the damage was to the passenger side and rear quarter. The bumper had fallen off and lay haphazardly in the ditch, amongst shards of red taillights and debris. *Should I pick that up and give it to him?*

I heard the police car siren before I saw its light. One patrol car, and then another, pulled up behind me on the soft shoulder of the road. Thankfully they killed the sirens as soon as they parked, but left the lights flashing.

I watched from my rear-view mirror as Officer McCutty stepped out, holding paper in his hand. *Him again!* Was I happy to see the somewhat familiar face or embarrassed to see him again so soon? It was hard to decipher my emotions.

He approached me and his partner went over to the other driver. I was glad he chose me.

I got out of my car once he was close.

"Elsie Lawson."

Should I be worried he remembered my name? But, then again, I just saw him last night. Maybe it'd been a slow day and he hadn't made a lot of traffic stops.

"Are you okay? Do you need an ambulance or medical attention?" he asked.

The image of me, on a stretcher, in a neck brace, being packed into the back of the ambulance popped into my mind. Heck no! "No, no, I don't think so." I was pretty sure I had bumps and bruises and didn't want to be fussed over.

He squinted at me. "You got red stuff all over your face—"

"It's soda," I said quickly.

"We'll still have an EMT check you out when they get here and make sure you're good."

"I'm okay, I think. My car is not." I looked at it for the first time since the accident happened and was shocked. My car's frame was oddly mangled, resting against a telephone pole. It was strangely surreal—like how did that happen when five minutes ago everything was perfectly fine? Imagine if he'd hit me on the driver's door of my car instead of the back. What would've happened? Would I have been injured? Would I have survived?

He handed me a clipboard to fill out an accident report. I went back to my car to get out of the biting air and wrote down the details as I remembered them. I added a quick sketch, including a compass (out of habit) in the area provided.

Once I handed him back the paperwork, he looked it over briefly. "Nice compass. Never had someone do that before."

"Sorry," I said, for no reason at all.

"Don't apologize, just a nicely-drawn detail. Now, why don't you tell me what happened."

I recounted the sequence of events as I remembered them and he scribbled down notes. I even added that when I saw the other car careening out of control, time seemed to slow. And how I could almost imagine the classical music that would go along with the scene, like in a figure skating competition or in a meme. Why I said that, I didn't know. I realized I probably wasn't making much sense to him.

The wail of another siren echoed in my ears and in the distance an ambulance approached.

He took my license, registration and insurance info back to the police cruiser while the EMT checked me out.

I returned to sit in my car, with the door open, as I answered the EMT's questions and then watched as Officer McCutty took pictures of the accident.

He pointed to the damaged part of the car. "You're going to have to repair more than just the tail light."

I went and stood beside him. I stared at the mangled steel formerly known as my car. "Yeah."

"I already called a tow truck."

I hadn't considered that. "Do you think I need one?"

He didn't even glance up. "Sorry, but yeah."

How do I get home? The idea of not being able to drive myself back to my parent's house overwhelmed me for a second. *What should I do?* I stared at my phone, figuring out who to call, which seemed far more difficult than it should've been. I didn't have to think too long because it didn't even turn on. *That's right! The battery's dead!*

Walking home was an option. It wasn't *that* far. Two miles, maybe. I could use the exercise given the big meal that was about to be served. That's what I'd do, it was the solution that made sense. Although I couldn't help feeling like a kid whose parents forgot to pick them up from school.

I waited by my car as McCutty talked to the other officer. The other driver approached. He looked unscathed and completely professional in his dark wool overcoat, Burberry scarf, sunglasses and leather gloves. It was a far cry from my pajama pants, oversized hoodie and sneakers. I could only imagine what he thought of me, looking like a couch potato.

He put a gloved-hand lightly on my forearm. "Are you okay?" His intense look, with his intense eyes, was unsettling. It was so...intense.

I stared at him, overwhelmed for a second by his good looks—dark wavy hair and deep brown eyes with flecks of gold, cheek bones, square jaw and sexy lips—the whole package.

His put-together manner made me feel even more scattered. How could he remain so calm and collected when we'd just been skidding on the road like a puck in a hockey game? I nodded excessively. "Yeah, yeah, I think so. Just a little shook up." I glanced behind him at his car. "Is your car okay?" The SUV looked a little banged up, but not as bad as mine. His damage was mostly to the passenger-side door. Should I retrieve his bumper now?

"It'll have to be repaired, but it's still drivable."

"That's good, I guess."

"You're not going to sue me, are you?" he asked.

I looked up at him, and then over at his car. What a mess.

And then my heart stopped as I read the lettering across the back lift gate of his car.

Lamborghini.

I was really bad at knowing car brands or recognizing the different models, but I knew what a Lamborghini was and that they were *really* expensive.

Technically it was his fault, since he hit me, but maybe since I took a right on red, it was my fault and...he drove a Lamborghini. There was no way I'd be able to win a lawsuit or pay for damages if he sued me. His scarf alone probably cost more than I earned in one week.

He added a smile (for good measure?), his gleaming teeth all even and straight. A little too perfect. Were they veneers?

"No. I don't plan to sue," I said.

He reached into his coat and pulled out something and handed it to me. "Here's my business card."

I took the it and rubbed my finger across it. It was black, thick, slick and embossed. It had weight to it and it was the nicest business card I'd ever seen.

Maddox Wellington.

I stared at the card. Maddox Wellington? Like Beef Wellington? I started laughing. Maybe his family were the original inventors of Beef Wellington. Could it be? Would he cook it for me some night?

His brow creased. "Is something…funny?"

"No. Sorry. I think I'm in shock." I turned my attention back to his card, pretending to examine it. The only other information on it was an email address. It provided very little insight about this guy.

He obviously did something that paid for his expensive sunglasses, expensive teeth, expensive gloves and his expensive car. But what?

"Do you have a card?" he asked.

"I do. Hold on."

I climbed into my car and searched through the random spilled contents of my purse until I found one. It too had Code Red splatter, but it was the only one I had. "Here you go," I said, handing it to him.

He glanced at it. "Elsie Lawson, freelance illustrator."

"Yes."

"I see you have Nevada plates. Did you move here from there?"

"Just visiting my parents for the holidays."

"Do you have a local address?" he asked.

Yes. But I wasn't about to give it to him. "No."

"But your parents live here, in Warren?"

I nodded. I didn't understand his curiosity and wasn't about to give him more information than he needed. "You have my card with my number on it. If you need to contact me, you can call." I glanced at his. "And I can...email." I held the card up. "No phone number?"

"Email is the best way to contact me."

After his answer, I was glad I didn't give him my local address. He could have my number but I couldn't have his? Weird. I wanted to snatch my sticky card back from him, but he still gripped it in his glove. *It'd be fine*, I told myself. Usually there wasn't contact between accident victims, since the insurance companies dealt with the two parties. *It'd be fine*.

"Are you sure you're okay?" he asked one more time.

Those five words opened the floodgates. "I don't know. I don't know what I'm going to do! My car is...ruined. My life is...a mess. And, I can't afford a new car, so now...I'm stuck here and—" I shook my head, trying to get a hold of my emotions. "Sorry. I'm sorry." I squeezed my eyes shut, but the tears still escaped.

He took a step closer, but I held up my hand. "I'm fine. Really. I'm fine. I'll be okay." I cleared my throat, wiped my eyes and squared my shoulders. I would pull myself together.

"Is there anything I can do for you?" he asked.

"Not unless you can buy me a new car," I muttered.

It was like he was frozen to the ground. He cocked his head and looked at me, with those piercing, dark eyes. I was embarrassed for my outburst and tears and just wanted him stop watching me. I didn't know what he expected of me.

"Well, thank you," I said, trying to move things along. *Thank you?* What a stupid thing to say! Why was I thanking him? I really just wanted to get out of the uncomfortable situation and have him go back to his car. After a few more beats, he gave me a nod and retreated to his side of the accident.

4

I sat on the cold curb as the tow truck pried my car off the pole. A hiccup turned into a small sob and within seconds, tears stung my eyes. Oh! I took measured breaths, willing myself to calm down.

With an ear-piercing scrape and a metal-bending groan, the chains on the truck dragged my car closer and closer to the flatbed. Alien-green liquid dripped from underneath the carriage, as well as a viscous, red leak that muddled the neon fluid into a strawberry milkshake-colored sludge.

My car looked like a steel fortune cookie crying strange tears of protest as the winch slowly pulled it higher and higher on the sloped ramp of the truck. An acrid scent hit me like smelling salts, causing another wave of tears.

Oh, my gosh! There was no way my car could be fixed. Look at it! It was dead.

My throat became thick with emotion and I blinked back tears. Maybe it wasn't just the awful scent causing the tears. I pressed the palms of my hands against my eyelids, trying to stop from crying.

I didn't have a car. I couldn't get back to Las Vegas. And

my roommate recently moved in with her boyfriend, so I needed to find a new roommate or a new apartment by December first. If I didn't, I couldn't even live in my car.

What am I going to do?

I swiped at my eyes and used my arm to wipe away my sniffles. I breathed through my mouth, hoping to calm down. If I could just regulate my breathing, maybe I could rein in my emotions. I felt ridiculous sitting on a curb, crying about my beater car.

It was just a car. Cars could be replaced. I was lucky I walked away from it unscathed because it could've been so much worse.

But I couldn't live without it. And I couldn't afford another one. Not right now at least.

Thoughts hurled at me that I was emotionally unable to dodge, and my stomach clenched so hard I felt like I was going to throw up.

Once Officer McCutty finished up, he clapped his hand on the shoulder of the other officer and walked over to me.

He studied me. "You okay?"

"Yes," I lied.

"Sure?"

"Absolutely," I lied again.

He stared at me long enough for me to wipe my eyes one more time to make sure there weren't any remaining tears. I just wanted to go home.

He handed me back my license and registration and a long, narrow strip of paper, like a receipt. "Here's a print-off of the accident details, your info, his info. You can pick up a complete accident report at the police station after this date. He pointed to a date that had been circled in pen. "And here's my badge number and the station number if you need to call me."

"Okay."

"Any questions?"

My mind drew a blank. "If I have any questions, I have your number."

"Don't hesitate to use it," he said.

I looked at him, our eyes met, and he nodded. Instantly, I had some questions. Did he want me to call it? Only about questions related to the accident, or for other questions? And what other questions would I have that I'd feel the need to call him? What was wrong with me and why was I reacting to him like this? I had to be in shock.

"Is someone coming to pick you up?"

I thumbed in the direction of home. "I'm going to walk."

"You didn't call anyone to come get you?" His tone reflected his surprise.

I held up my phone as if it were proof. "My phone's dead, but it's okay," I said quickly, forcing a smile. "I can walk. It's just off Water Street."

"My shift is ending. I'll give you a lift."

I looked around at the other police officer on scene, wondering if McCutty was breaking some sort of rule. "Are you allowed to do that?" Where would I sit? I hadn't ever been in the back of a police car before and I wanted to keep it that way.

"Of course. And, if you want, I can even knock on your front door and make it seem like you got in trouble." He winked and gave me a half-smile.

"I don't know if that would be a great joke or lead to a lecture." Even though I sounded hesitant, I wasn't *that* hesitant.

He held up his left hand and shook it. "I'm not looking to get you in trouble. If you really want, I'll drop you off at the corner."

I had exaggerated a little. I was a grown adult and if I got a ride home from a police officer, it didn't mean I was in trouble.

"I'll take the ride and let you drop me off at the house." It was cold and I really, really didn't want to walk home. I collected my personal items from my car and returned to where Officer McCutty waited.

"Ready?" he asked. "Everyone's probably waiting on you at the dinner table." He opened the back door of the cruiser. Sort of like a perfect gentleman.

"I have to sit in the back?" I was horrified. I blinked back another wave of tears that stung my eyes. I wasn't a *criminal*. I'd convinced myself that he'd let me ride up front with him.

He shrugged. "Protocol."

Like I could argue with a cop. That would surely get me arrested for something. Then I'd *really* have something to cry about. I didn't want to earn my place in the back seat, so, without further protest, I slid into the hard plastic backseat. Yuck! It felt so . . . horrible in here. And what kind of germs were on these seats? I sniffed the air. It didn't smell like a drunk person, but it didn't smell like Lysol, either. I hoped they cleaned and sanitized these surfaces regularly.

The silence weighed on me and I felt compelled to start a conversation with him. But he was a police officer and I guessed they generally didn't want to be chatted up. Was it even a good idea to try and chat him up? Not in the flirty way, of course. In the trying-to-make-conversation-because-it's-just-the-two-of-us-in-a-police-car kind of way. Was I even capable of carrying on a conversation without starting to bawl like a big baby? Maybe it was better if I just kept my mouth shut.

He broke the ice. "Big family dinner?" he asked, making eye contact in the rear-view mirror.

"Sorry?"

"Thanksgiving. Are you having a big family dinner?"

I cleared my throat. "Uh, yeah."

"I better hurry and get you home. Want me to turn on the lights?"

Oh. My. Gosh! That was all I needed. Arriving home in a police car with the lights on would be the talk of the meal. "And the siren?" I asked half-heartedly.

Was that a hint of a smile I saw pass over his face?

"That might be a bit over-the-top, don't you think?" he said. He looked back over his shoulder and I could see a grin on his face. He was joking. I exhaled. I felt a smidge better knowing he had a sense of humor.

"Maybe you should drop me off at the corner of Water Street," I said. That would soften the arrival home and be way less dramatic.

He made eye contact again by the rear-view mirror. "And miss all the fun? No way."

He must've known the commotion he would cause by delivering me home via police car.

"Besides," he continued. "I wouldn't want you slipping on ice. Black ice has already wreaked havoc in your life once."

I swallowed hard. "That's very...considerate of you," I said.

"I'm here to serve," he said, that smile reflecting in the mirror again. I liked his smile, framed by his cute lips.

His cute lips? Where did that come from? I'm in shock. It's because I'm in shock.

"These seats are very uncomfortable," I said, shifting around to try and get comfortable. It wasn't a long ride, but that hard plastic made it feel longer.

"They're supposed to be. Imagine being cuffed, too."

I imagined it, for a second, and then shook the image from my mind. "I hope I'm never in the back seat of a cruiser again."

His eyebrows lifted. "Again?"

"I mean, after this ride," I quickly corrected. "I've never been in a police car before."

"Good to hear."

He pulled onto Water Street. I silently watched the familiar scenery go by as I wondered what was going to happen with my car. Was I stuck here for now? What sort of chatter would happen at dinner because a police officer brought me home?

"What's the address?"

I rattled off my parents' address.

"I know exactly where that is. I live close by."

Suddenly it all made sense. Driving me home was on his way home. Not him flirting with that cute smile, but a convenient pit-stop before heading home.

My emotions dropped a little. I thought he'd been flirting.

5

As soon as Officer McCutty pulled up to my house, parking in front of the driveway and essentially blocking it off, the curtain from the kitchen window flitted. Someone knew I was home. Either they'd been watching for me, or just happened to look out at the window at the exact moment we drove in. I chose the former.

"Here we go," I said under my breath.

"Did you say something?" he asked.

I shook my head. "Just that someone knows I'm home." I went to open the door, only to discover there was no handle. Well, of course there'd be no handle. That would only make it easier for the criminals to escape.

I waited for him to open the door for me. That, in and of itself, made me look guilty of something. Getting into a car accident while chasing down sweet potatoes didn't seem like a big enough crime.

I barely set foot on the snowy ground before the front door flung open and Mom, Vivian, Max and Miley burst out. Nana watched from the window; the curtain now completely pushed aside.

"What's wrong?" Mom cried out, as if I'd been gone for hours with no word.

"Why are you in a police car?" Miley asked, eyes wide.

"Can I go in the police car?" Max asked. I kind of hoped Officer McCutty would say yes, and it would lessen my being in the car. Then it'd be like a fun activity, exploring the police car, maybe getting a ride around the block, possibly with the lights on. Kind of like what Auntie Elsie did.

"I had a car accident," I said.

"You had a car accident?" Miley shouted loud enough for the whole neighborhood to hear.

"Are you okay?" Vivian asked.

Mom took a few steps toward me. "Honey." Her tone had softened. She reached out and brushed her palm across my cheek.

Her touch triggered the tears. I nodded and cleared my throat of the emotion gathering in it. "I think my car is totaled." I swiped at my eyes.

"Your car is totaled?" Max repeated. "What does 'totaled' mean?"

"It means she's really in trouble," Miley explained, acting as if she really knew what was going on.

"Oh," Max said, eyes wide, as if he understood *how* much trouble I was really in.

"Why didn't you call?" my mom asked, her tone implying that it was the obvious thing to do, which it was.

I held my hands up in frustration, then quickly shoved them back in my coat pockets because it was so cold. "My phone died."

"Hi, Officer McCutty," Vivian said, looking past my shoulder. Did I detect a note of flirtation in her voice?

"Oh, hey, Vivian. I didn't know you two were sisters."

How did he know Vivian's name? And why was she flirting with him?

Before I could respond, Nana shuffled to the front door. "I saw all this hugging and thought I needed to join."

Officer McCutty took a couple of steps backwards. "Well, I'll leave you folks alone. Happy Thanksgiving."

I turned to him. "Thank you. I appreciate your help," I said.

"Thanks for bringing her home safely," Nana called.

"That is so cool that he drove you home," Vivian whispered as we closed the front door.

"Yeah, all cool except for the part where I was in a car accident." I retorted.

Vivian pulled a frowny face. "Yeah, that does suck."

Yeah, like a lot. A little more than she realized. I'd probably be stranded here until I could scrape enough money together to buy a new car, since I didn't have an apartment any more in Vegas. And although hanging out with my family through the holidays would be cool and fun and all, we all had our limitations. Sometimes, "more" time turned into "too much" time. And I didn't want it to get to the point where it was too much time.

"But he's Officer McCutey. If there's a positive, that's it." My sister's tone sounded like she was pointing out the obvious.

"How do you have a nickname for him?" I thought her name for him was cute. And fitting. Especially since I had called him the same thing. Although Maddox Wellington wasn't half-bad himself.

"He comes into Dunkin's all the time."

"You still work there?" I asked. "I thought you planned to quit when the semester started."

She shrugged. "I changed my mind."

Mom called for help to finish the final preparations for dinner. No one asked about sweet potatoes and, in my opinion, they weren't even missed.

Melissa insisted I take a "mild" painkiller that she had dug out from the bottom of her purse and that I would "thank her later". I took it without question, which might've been a mistake. Thanksgiving dinner was a blur of pass the turkey, more mashed potatoes, the gravy is delicious, that's a beautiful...float it's in... Is it an heir...worm...? After that, it all became a little hazy.

6

"Elsie!" Vivian yelled.

Why is she yelling?

She sounded far away, in the distance. Maybe I was dreaming it. What was I dreaming anyway? I blinked my eyes open, only to see my sister's face directly in front of mine. What was she doing? Why was she doing that? Where was I anyway?

I pulled my face off the pillow, where I was more than likely drooling since the fabric was stuck to my cheek, and sat up. "Ow! Ow! Ow!" I cried. My neck!

"Elsie!" my sister called out again.

My head was foggy and hair was in my face and I felt like I'd been hit by a Mack truck. Or a Lamborghini. I was stiff, my muscles sore, and my neck hurt when I straightened it.

"What?" I sat up as my eyes popped open. "Ow!" I cried, rubbing the back of my neck. I tested it again, slowly turning it to the right, and the sharp pain stabbed me again. It sadly hadn't disappeared in the last thirty seconds. "Ow, ow, ow, ow!" I'd never had whiplash before, but was pretty sure I had it now.

"What time is it?" I asked. I started to look behind me, but immediately stopped because of the pain.

"It's 8:30."

"At night?" It wasn't dark enough to be nighttime.

"No. Friday morning."

Friday morning? "Did I sleep through Thanksgiving? Did my Troy and Melissa already leave? Are there any leftover pies?"

"Yes, yes and no. Troy and Melissa took the pies with them."

"They left?" I hadn't even gotten to say goodbye to them. Or have pie.

"Yup. You passed out."

I must've. I held my arms out and I was wearing the same clothes from yesterday, just more crumpled. Whatever Melissa gave me, it completely knocked me out. Even enough that I didn't notice how uncomfortable the horrible sofa was while I slept.

"But I know something that will cheer you up. She grabbed my hand. "Follow me," she said.

With great care, I stood, trying not to strain my neck. I found I couldn't move at normal speed and had to slow down to geriatric speed. Instead of attempting to pull on my hoodie, I grabbed my bathrobe and pulled it on, hurrying as fast as my sore body could move to find out what all the excitement was.

"Just kill me now," I moaned, wishing she wasn't rushing me.

"Trust me, you won't want to die when you see this," Vivian said, oblivious to the pain I was experiencing.

Her enthusiasm was admirable, but the pain she caused

was not. I stopped and shook myself from her grasp. "Stop, stop. My body is killing me. Literally, it is in a lot of pain from the accident yesterday."

She took a step back. "Oh. Sorry. But hurry!"

The smell of bacon permeated the air, wafting in from the kitchen. And while bacon was great and all, that had better not be what she was excited about. I mean, we just ate it yesterday.

I shuffled behind her, wondering if Advil would take care of my aches and pains. Would I need to make a trip to the Quick Care and get a prescription for something a little stronger than Advil but not as strong as my sister-in-law's prescribed medicine?

Mom, Dad and Nana were gathered by the front door, which was opened. Mom stepped to the right to make room for me, revealing a man standing there.

"This is Elsie," Mom said.

"These are yours," the man said, handing me a set of keys and a thick, business-sized envelope.

I held them up. "What are these for?" I asked.

"That," he said and pointed to the driveway.

Now I understood what all the fuss was about.

Outside was a shiny, new, silver car with a big, red bow that covered the entire roof.

I clutched the envelope. "That's mine?!"

"Yup."

I grabbed the man and hugged him (and, thanks to my neck, instantly regretted it). "Thank you! Thank you!"

He untangled himself from my grasp. "You're welcome, but I'm just the delivery guy."

I turned to my parents. "You guys bought me a new car?" I couldn't believe it! I threw myself into my mother's arms (and had a repeat of regret). My dad never bought new cars nor did he put much thought into gift-giving. My poor mom had never had a new car in her life. This was so out of character for them and definitely the most expensive gift they'd ever given me.

Had my parents had a windfall of money that I didn't know about? That might explain this oddly-grand-gesture-thing going on right now.

I mean, it was possible. I didn't know all of their business.

My answer was two blank stares.

I looked from Mom to Dad. I didn't understand.

"I didn't buy that car," Dad said. He sounded just as confused as I was.

Was brain whiplash a thing? Clearly, I had no clue what was happening.

"Then who did?" I asked.

"You might want to check the paperwork," the delivery man said, then took two steps back. "You folks have a nice day."

"Thank you!" I called out after him as he walked to a car waiting for him.

"Who just gives someone a car?" Vivian asked.

"I don't know," I murmured.

But I had my suspicions. Maybe someone who could afford to drive a Lamborghini. But no. I quickly dismissed my idea. It couldn't be. But could it? I tore open the envelope searching for a bill of sale or a clue. Anything. But there wasn't any information.

"Maybe there's a note on the car?" Mom suggested.

Mom, Vivian, and even Dad, pulled on their winter coats and rushed to the driveway.

I decided my bathrobe would be warm enough, slipped into my boots (quite a task when you can't look down or bend over) and shuffled outside, clutching the keys.

The cold air punched my lungs, making it hard to breathe. My bathrobe was definitely *not* warm enough.

Vivian walked around the car, searching for a clue, while Mom and Dad stood on either side of the front end, admiring the vehicle.

It was a four-door Honda Accord with shiny hubcaps, undented bumpers and a pristine paint job. I pressed my face against the cold window on the driver's side (carefully) to peek inside.

"Let's go for a ride!" Vivian squealed.

I pressed the key fob and the car greeted me with the happy sound of doors unlocking. Even as I slid into the leather seat and rested my hands on the steering wheel, I wondered how could this be mine. *There's got to be a mistake.*

Vivian held up an envelope sticking out of the cup holder. "Here's your answer."

I slipped my finger under the seal and read the printed message.

For the damsel in distress.

—*Maddox Wellington.*

Of course, he was responsible for the car. He had to be responsible for the car. Who else could afford to give away a brand-new car?

"Well," Vivian demanded. "Did you find anything out?"

I nodded. "The mystery has been solved."

Mom, Dad and Vivian all leaned in closer.

"And?" Vivian asked.

I showed them the card. "It's from the guy I had the accident with yesterday," I said.

"Who exactly did you hit?" Mom asked. "Bill Gates?"

I held up my index finger. "First, he hit me. Second, his

name is Maddox Wellington. Third, he is much, *much* better looking than Bill Gates."

"Maddox Wellington." My dad repeated the name, thoughtfully. "I've heard about him. Isn't he the guy who wants to bring his business here?"

I shrugged. "I don't know. We didn't talk business, just exchanged information. And then he bought me a car," I said as an afterthought.

Vivian shrieked. "Holy cow! It's your car! C'mon! We've got to take it out for a spin."

"Should we take the bow off first?" I asked, not knowing what to do. Was I supposed to leave it on? Take it off?

"Let's drive around with it on. Like *Just Married*, but *Just Gifted*!" Vivian exclaimed.

"Don't leave without me!" Nana yelled from the front porch.

Vivian jumped out of the car to help Nana, and I admired my newly-gifted jackpot. I put the key in the ignition and turned. It started! My warm breath fogged up the cold glass as I exhaled. The navigation system and the lights on the dashboard came to life in the twinkling of an eye. I ran my hand over the stereo, touched all the buttons for all the systems, taking it all in. Thrilled was an understatement. But more than that, grateful.

With my curiosity satisfied, I put the car into drive.

With my hands at "10" and "2", I gripped the steering wheel, creeping down the street at a snail's pace.

"Why so slow, Elsie?" Vivian asked when I pulled onto Water Street. She looked over her shoulder. "There's a whole row of cars behind us."

I adjusted the rearview mirror so I could get a proper look. There wasn't a *whole row*, just three. "I'm trying to get a feel for the car. I haven't driven it before."

Actually, I wanted to pull over to let the others pass. Having cars behind me pressured me, making me feel like I needed to speed up. And I didn't want to. What if I hit a patch of ice like the other car did yesterday? I didn't want to slide off the road, or into another car, or another telephone pole.

Luckily, the cars turned off before we made it to the light. I could've taken a right on red, but decided against it. I needed to be extra careful driving, especially—

Beep! Beep! Beeeeep!

"You drive slower than me, and I'm not allowed to drive anymore," Nana said.

"Go, Elsie," Vivian urged.

I looked up to see the light had changed.

A tail of the red ribbon fell onto the windshield as I turned. My automatic response was to turn on the windshield wipers, hoping to sweep it out of my sight line. It only aggravated the situation, pulling it down farther.

Should I stop and take it off? I couldn't keep driving with that huge bow sliding all over my windshield, could I?

A chirp of a siren snapped me out of my fixation.

Again?

It was a brand-new car. I knew I didn't have a tail light out.

I took the next right turn and stopped. Once again, I watched in the rearview mirror, dreading who would emerge from the police SUV. Silently, and secretly, I hoped it'd be Officer McCutty. By now, he had to know I was a law-abiding citizen just trying to drive from point A to point B safely.

I recognized, and privately rejoiced, when the now-familiar face of Officer McCutty got out.

I rolled down my window and stuck my head out. "Hi," I said meekly.

He offered me a smile. "We've got to stop running into each other this way."

"What way?" I wondered what exactly he meant. Like while he was working? While I was driving?

"On the side of the road with my lights on behind you."

"Maybe the next time we meet, you won't be working," I said without thinking. That sounded like I wanted to see him outside of work. Had I hit my head in the accident? I couldn't exactly remember if I had, and when I tried to recall, it was sort of a blur. How would he respond? Would he say something like 'I'd like that?' or 'I get off at six'.

Nana rolled down the back window and stuck both hands out. "If joyriding's a crime, arrest me right now," she said.

"Nana!" I hissed. "Arms in the window. He's not going to arrest you."

"Maybe he's going to arrest *you*," she said. She sounded oddly cheerful.

"I didn't do anything wrong, did I?" At least, not that I was aware of. Why *had* I been pulled over?

"It's more of a precaution. Your big, red bow looked like it was going to fly off."

I was pretty sure my cheeks burned as bright as that big, red bow. Of course, that was the reason. I wasn't skating under *anyone's* radar with that thing on top of my car. And certainly not his.

Vivian leaned forward to see around me. "Elsie was given this car today by guy she got in the accident with. We had to try it out."

Officer McCutty clucked his tongue. "Well, who better to get into an accident with than a billionaire?"

My ears perked up and my heart did a weird stutter thing. "What?"

"Maddox Wellington is a billionaire."

"He's rich?" I asked, but then thought about it. Like I even had to wonder. Look at the car he drove.

"He bought you a car, didn't he?" Officer McCutty said.

Of course, he was rich. It only made sense.

But a billionaire?

"You sure he's a billionaire? Like, with a B?" I asked.

"With a B."

"Oh," I said, stunned.

"Way to go Elsie! Get into an accident with a billionaire," Vivian said. The congratulatory way she said it made it seem like I'd achieved something great.

"Trust me, it was not on purpose," I said.

"You know who he is, right?" Officer McCutty said.

No. Apparently, I didn't. My blank stare must've given my ignorance away.

"Google him," he said. "You'll see."

"I'm on it right now," Vivian said, quickly tapping away on her phone.

"Before I let you go, you're going to either have to take the bow off, or secure it better," he said.

"That's it?" Nana said. Now she sounded disappointed. "You're not going to search me—I mean—the car or anything?"

When did Nana turn into such a flirt? Either that, or she was really bored in her life and was looking for some excitement. Any kind of excitement.

Officer McCutty cleared his throat. "No need to do that," he said.

Vivian poked her head out like a turtle to see him.

"Thanks, Officer McCutty. Next time you're in the drive thru, coffee's on me," she said.

"Thanks, Vivian," he said. "You ladies take care, now."

Not wanting to take any chances, Vivian and I took the bow off the roof and jammed it in the trunk. It was like wrestling an octopus. I hated to ruin such a fun decoration, but didn't want to start off my new car ownership with a ticket.

After our run-in with the law, we cut our outing short and headed home.

Joyriding was definitely less fun, and less pretentious, with the bow off.

7

As I drove, Vivian filled us in on the billionaire by reading off his Wikipedia page. "It says here that Maddox Wellington, Dawson Carter, Preston Carter, Brooks Stansfield and Benedict Harxly developed the app, 4you2, while in college and launched it five years ago. Deemed the next Facebook, the company's net worth is roughly one hundred and fifty billion dollars. Maddox has left the company but retains a position as a consultant, focusing his efforts on property development now. His net worth is 6.9 billion." Vivian took a large, exaggerated inhale. "Wow. He's a legit billionaire."

That just made him officially more intimidating.

Once home, I pulled out the business card Maddox Wellington had given me. Sending an email as a thank you for such a huge gift felt wildly inappropriate and not enough. The new information I'd learned from Officer McCutty and Vivian overshadowed my ability to write what should've been a pretty straight-forward message.

A bunch of questions flooded my mind as I gripped the card, picking at the corner. I mean, did he give me the car free and clear? If he was as rich as Officer McCutty claimed he was, he surely could afford it. Did he buy the car with a down payment and I was expected to make the rest of the payments? I couldn't really afford that right now and couldn't take on any debt. But I also needed a car since I was pretty sure my car was totaled. Could I accept such a generous gift from a stranger? I was leaning toward *YES!!!!!!!*

The blood pounded in my ears. I had no reason to be nervous, but he was good-looking and he was intimidating in that overly-confident way. And a billionaire. But that shouldn't matter. I should look at the situation the way it really was: he was an ordinary man, who caused an accident, and was trying to fix the damage. Only, he wasn't an ordinary man, he was a billionaire, and this wasn't an ordinary thing he did to correct the situation. I mean, who goes out and gifts a brand-new car to a stranger? Really? Who does that? Apparently, billionaires, that's who. It was such a weird situation. I didn't know what to do: accept or return the car. Only one way to find out.

Dear Maddox Wellington, I typed, then stopped. ...too formal.

Delete, delete, delete.

Hey, Maddox...too casual

More backspacing.

Mr. Wellington...still too formal. Why was I referring to him as "Mr."? He looked about the same age as me.

Finally, I skipped the salutation and forced myself to type out a heartfelt thank you, making sure I conveyed my appreciation for his over-the-top generosity. I decided to wait on all of my questions until I sent this. That way the thank you could be separate and not muddled with all my anxieties that came with such a gift.

I hit send, dropped my phone and fell back against the

couch, forgetting about my pain. But my pain didn't forget about me and reminded me quickly not to do that again. "Ow, ow ow!"

My phone vibrated beside me.

Random private number: So, it's okay?

Me: Who is this?

Random private number: Maddox Wellington

Me: How did you get my number?

Maddox: You gave me your business card.

Oh, yeah, I'd forgotten about that.

Me: Yes, I got the car! Thank you!! Did you get my email? I just barely hit send.

Maddox: Yes. Do you like it?

Did I like it? What kind of question was that?

Me: Yaaaas!

I'd never been gifted such an expensive gift. Heck, I'd never even had a new car before.

Me: It's really mine?

Maddox: Yes

I was literally speechless. And textless. How should I respond?

Me: Oh, my gosh! Thanks so much!!! I can't believe it!

Maddox: You're welcome.

And I couldn't imagine how much extra that big red bow on top must've cost.

Maddox: There is one condition.

My stomach dropped. *I knew it!* There was something. Nothing was ever truly "free". Was I going to be hit with a huge tax bill or something? My fingers hovered over the phone before I finally got the courage to type a response.

Me: What is it?

I held my breath.

Maddox: ...

The little bubbles danced in synchronized succession.

Was he thinking? Or just typing a really long response?

While I waited, I created a contact for him and found, what I thought, was an appropriate ring tone. I chose "Money, Money, Money" by Abba.

I didn't know how much he was typing, but it took almost ten minutes to hear back from him.

My phone lit up as my new "Money, Money, Money" ringtone blared.

The random, PRIVATE number, which belonged to Maddox Wellington, appeared.

My heart jumped into my throat. Oh, my gosh! He was calling me! What should I say? At least with texting I could think before I typed. Talking to him was a whole different situation.

I stabbed at my green phone icon.

"Good afternoon," he said, his voice sounding smooth and creamy like he hadn't just woken up and dragged himself out of bed.

I cleared my throat. "Hi," I said, unsure. I rubbed my hand across the scratchy surface of the ugly Victorian couch, which had absolutely no soothing abilities whatsoever. I stood up and paced around the perimeter of the room. "Thank you for the car, again. It's perfect."

"I tried to get the same thing as what you were driving." He paused. "Only newer."

My car was fifteen years old. But he nailed the color, albeit it not so dull from age. "I, uh, no. I'm...a little taken aback. I mean, who does that?" *That's crazy!*

There was an audible chuckle. "I guess I do."

"What's the condition?"

"That's why I called," he said. "Hold on, please. I've got a call." The phone clicked into silence, leaving me in curiosity limbo.

Here it was. The one hiccup that would ruin the gift. Take over the payments? Pay him back when I could? Be his love slave? Okay, I doubted he'd want me to be his love slave. Besides, I was against slavery.

I held my breath and waited.

He clicked back seconds later. "Go out to dinner with me," he said.

That...was...unexpected. "You mean a date?" I asked once I was able to piece together a coherent sentence.

"Exactly." It sounded like he was smiling.

If that was the only condition as a thank you, I could definitely handle that. I'm sure it was just an extra precaution that we were "good". I did a little happy dance, which I instantly regretted. That was an easy condition to accept. "I'd love to."

"Great. How soon can you be ready?"

What? "You mean today?"

"Sure. Why not?"

I staggered back into an arm chair, once again jarring my neck from (slight) impact. *Ow! Ow! Ow!* "No! I can't!" I blurted out. *Crap! Why did I say that?* That's not what I meant. Dang it! Whiplash seemed to have affected my brain as well.

"No?" The surprise in his voice was obvious.

Did he get told "no" very often? "I need more time. To plan. To get ready."

"You're not the spontaneous type?"

I wouldn't say that exactly. I could be spontaneous, just not today. "Don't you have whiplash or anything from yesterday?"

"I'm a little sore," he said. "Nothing some Advil can't take care of."

I pictured the airbags in his Lamborghini swelling up around him like a gentle bubble, protecting him from even the slightest amount of impact. In fact, cushioning him like memory foam. "Well, me too. And my neck hates me. I'd love to go out with you, but I'd like to be able to turn my head first." *Then I could gaze into his beautiful, brown eyes.*

Stop it!

"What can I do for you? Send over a masseuse? I know a great one and she makes house calls."

That sounded wrong in several ways, none of which I wished to address with him. "I don't know," I hedged.

"Don't try to get out of it. I'm persistent," he said, teasing.

Why would I try and get out of it? What was not to like about a gorgeous billionaire? Hard for me to find anything wrong with that equation. And I'd need my neck in good, working order if I was going to kiss him. *Where did that come from?*

"It's not that. I smell like an old person," I blurted out.

"You smell like an old person?" he asked. "Is that from mothballs or something?"

Why couldn't he text like every other Millennial? Talking in person made it hard to take back whatever silly thing I had just said.

"I used Nana's Ben Gay. She uses it on her bad knees," I explained. Surely, he had to know what Ben Gay smelled like. "That's why later tonight would be better."

"I can do later. How about tonight?" He was so cheerful.

I hated him a tiny bit for feeling so good after the accident. Why couldn't I feel just as good?

"Could you do after seven?" he asked.

Not smelling like I do right now.

I paused and took a breath. I didn't want to blurt out my answer, which was obviously a "yes". I wanted to sound more composed than a giddy girl. "I think so," I said calmly.

Honestly, I didn't really know what to think other than: *did Ben Gay wash off easily in the shower?* How do you be with a guy who is *that* rich? He's on a totally different level in life and it caused total and complete intimidation on my part.

He was persistent. And probably relentless. If he was that insistent, I should go. It wasn't like there'd be another date. Sort of like a hit-and-run sort of relationship. I'd probably never hear from him again, so why not? "Okay."

His phone clicked. "Excuse me for just a minute. I've got to take this call, but I'll be back in no time. I promise."

True to his word, he came back to our conversation almost immediately. "Sorry about that."

"No problem," I said.

"I have a conference call in exactly two minutes, so I'll have my personal assistant call you to set it up. When a number comes up as 'PRIVATE', make sure you answer it, okay?"

Another 'PRIVATE' number. From now on, everything that came up as PRIVATE was an automatic answer.

"Okay," I said.

His personal assistant would call? He had a personal assistant? Why didn't he schedule his own dates? I supposed, since he was a billionaire, he naturally would have some sort of person to handle his personal matters.

I was *so* out of my league. My heart beat harder.

"I'm looking forward to spending time with you," he said, his voice smooth and velvety.

"Me, too," I squeaked out, not smooth and velvety.

As soon as we hung up, I started with the self-deprecation. 'Me, too?' I said aloud. "As if I'm looking forward to spending time with myself? What an *idiot* I am!" I found the closest pillow, pulled it over my face and screamed into it. Why? Why? Why? Couldn't I sound calm and collected instead of bumbling and idiotic? Just for once?!

My phone rang, interrupting my crazy, runaway thoughts. I sat up, felt the ping in my neck, regretted my actions, shoved the pillow away and pushed the hair off my face. PRIVATE showed up on my screen. I braced myself for this experience. It was the personal assistant. How hard could it be? Just like scheduling a doctor's appointment. Just without the nurse. And without the doctor.

"Hello," I said, reclaiming that calm voice I had attempted to use in my prior conversation.

"Elsie?" It was a man's voice. Clearly not the sexy, young female voice I anticipated. Or even the tinny, old-lady voice I'd hoped for.

"Yes?" Had I mistakenly answered a spam call, assuming it was from Maddox's secretary but it was really about my car's extended warranty? The car that had been totaled?

"This is Wilson. I'm Mr. Maddox's PA."

He was Maddox's personal assistant? Shouldn't he at least have a British accent and be named Alfred?

None of the clichés I'd conjured were right. "Hi," I managed.

"Are you available at seven tonight?"

Seven, eight, whenever. I was free. "Yes," I said.

"Mr. Wellington will pick you up at six." He repeated back my address, then paused and waited for my response.

"Yes, yes. I'll be ready!" My voice gave away my excitement. So much for calm, cool and collected. I was giddy, silly and completely anxious about my upcoming date.

8

After rushing through the shower, I popped a few more Advil since the stress made my neck worse. I didn't dare touch the muscle relaxers Melissa had left for me. I didn't want to be *that* relaxed. I pressed my fist into my stomach hoping to quell the anxiety. Nothing helped. It was still off the charts. For real.

I made my way to Vivian's room, planning on raiding her closet. She was home from school, but obviously not studying, since she was laying on her bed watching TV.

"Help!" I said.

She sat up immediately, as if I was bleeding out or something. "What's wrong?"

"I need to choose an outfit."

She flopped down. "Elsie, that's not an emergency."

"It's for a date with the billionaire," I said.

She sprung back up; her eyes wide. "Why didn't you say so! When did he ask you out?"

"A half-hour ago. And it's for tonight." Saying the words out loud made my stomach tighten with anticipation.

"What are you doing? That determines what you should wear."

"I know," I groaned. My expectations for our date were all over the place. Would he go for a low-key dinner? Would it be crazy fancy? Would it be on his private yacht (did he even own one? And, it was November) or would he whisk me off to some expensive restaurant in a fabulous city? I had no idea what to expect. "But I don't know what the plans are."

Vivian gave me a pointed look. "Well, text him and find out."

At her encouragement, and with her hovering over my shoulder, I texted him.

Me: What are we doing? I'm not sure how to dress.

Maddox: Something over the top. Wear something nicer.

Nicer? What did that mean? Obviously, nicer than what I was wearing for the accident.

Me: Casual? Formal?

Maddox: In between. Night out on the town.

He might be disappointed.

"What does 'nicer' mean? Little-black-dress kind of nice or formal-dress kind of nice?"

Vivian went to her closet, pushed aside a few hangers and produced a black dress. It buttoned down the front, had a tie waist and sheer long sleeves, and would definitely do the trick. I borrowed the dress and a pair of shoes (that were a little tight) from Vivian.

∽

THE SUN WAS SETTING as I watched out the window, anticipating if a limo or a vintage Rolls Royce with a driver (other than Maddox) would pick me up.

A car certainly did pick me up, and it wasn't either of my guesses. It was a Tesla, and Maddox was driving. He met me at the front door. "You look perfect."

I almost blurted out everything I felt was wrong with my outfit choice, but decided enjoy his compliment. My confidence surged. "Thank you. Where's the Lamborghini?" I asked.

"In the shop. They can't get to it for about two weeks. Not even for me."

"Is this your loaner? At least you didn't get stuck with a compact."

"Nah, I bought it. I needed something immediately and didn't want to wait around for insurance to give me permission."

That meant he bought two brand new cars in one week, possibly the same day. How would that be?

I relaxed and settled into the supple, leather seats as we left.

We drove to Newport, a town rife with wealth, both history and people. Would we visit the lavish mansions of the famous Vanderbilts? Maybe enjoy some seafood and a stroll down the cliff walk? My stomach twisted with excitement as I imagined possible activities. When we pulled into a small, private airport and I saw a helicopter, I had a moment of hesitation.

"Where are we going?" I asked before getting out of the car.

Anticipation for the evening gripped my stomach. It was excitement and anxiety all rolled up into one.

The way he smiled at me made me want to melt. "I

promised you over-the-top. We're going to fly over the city," he said.

"Are we going on a tour of Newport at night?" I asked.

His smile widened. "I thought we'd visit New York City. I mean, why not?"

Of course, we'd hop on a helicopter and head over to New York City. I mean, why not, indeed?

His arm hovered centimeters from my waist as we walked. Like he was guiding me without touching me. "Have you ever been in a helicopter?" he asked.

"Once. On a reality dating show. We went on a helicopter tour of Mount Kilauea." It was a once-in-a-lifetime experience seeing a live volcano; it was just unfortunate who I shared it with. But I was thankful I'd been on a helicopter ride before so I didn't have to stress about it now.

"So, you're an expert."

"Hardly," I said.

Maddox angled his head. "Tell me about this dating show."

We put on our headphones as the door was shut and the engine turned on.

I inhaled so much my rib cage visibly expanded. I managed a wobbly smile. "Well, I'm still single, so obviously I wasn't his Mrs. Right."

Maddox offered me a confident smile in return. "His loss."

"Do you usually travel by helicopter, private jet or fly commercial?" I asked, desperate to change the conversation.

"Sometimes, sometimes, and sometimes. I fly all different ways, it's usually what makes more sense. But honestly, commercial is my least favorite and private jet is my personal preference."

"Commercial isn't always the best, but it sure beats driving," I said.

"When do you drive back to Nevada?" he asked.

"After the holidays. At least that's the plan for now. How about you? Do you travel a lot for work?"

"Yes. How about you?"

I snorted. "I'm an artist. I can't afford to travel anywhere."

"That's right. Freelance illustrator."

I was impressed he remembered. "What do you do?" I wanted to hear his version of *him*.

"Have you ever heard of 4you2?"

"Of course."

"My buddies and I started that after college."

I already knew that, courtesy of my sister and Google. "But you're not the face of 4you2." Although with his face, he should be.

"Do you mean the president of it? Like Mark Zuckerberg for Facebook and Meta?"

"Yeah."

"I'm more of a consultant now. When I worked there full time, I was a developer. I did go to all the same meetings with Ben, the president, if that counts."

I knew who he meant. That's the person I thought of when I thought of 4you2. He also had a face worthy of being the "face" of 4you2.

"We all worked in the area we're best in."

"What do you do now that you only consult for 4you2?" I asked.

"I'm pursuing real estate development," he said.

"So why Warren?"

His brow creased. "What do you mean?"

"Why do you live in Warren? It's a tiny, little town full of restaurants and shops. It's not Silicon Valley."

"I live in Warren because that's where I found the house with the view I wanted. The founders of 4you2 chose this area because we all went to MIT and like it here. My company is researching the possibility of bringing some of 4you2's operation centers here. There's lots of manufacturing and commercial buildings that are abandoned or underdeveloped that we could potentially use for our business. We're really passionate about boosting local economies."

"How's the town's passion about bringing big business to our small town? Change takes a lot of time here."

He nodded slowly. "I'm finding that out."

The skyline of New York City came into to view. I turned my attention, and my head (carefully), to the window and took in the scenery. The city lights, the black shimmer of the ocean, it truly was magnificent. It was worth the neck pain to see the bright spots turn into familiar sights as we approached.

"If this is what you do for a first date, what you do for a second date?"

I knew this was just for fun. He was making up for the car accident. And I was only staying until Christmas. I wasn't going to fall in love in three weeks.

He smiled widely. "Want to find out?"

That was unexpected. My question really had been rhetorical. But, of course I did! That was a no-brainer. "Yes."

"Great. I'll start working on that."

A thought niggled at the back of my mind. What would I do when it was my turn to plan a date—if it even got that far? I stuffed that thought into the back of my mind. *Enjoy the moment.*

When we landed, a limo picked us up and we enjoyed champagne while being whisked off to dinner. We went to a tiny French restaurant at the top of a hotel with views overlooking Times Square. It had really big prices and amazing food, some that I couldn't even pronounce. I literally had to point at the menu to order. Classy, I know.

After dinner we did a sightseeing tour of New York City in the helicopter.

"Do you do this with all your dates?" I asked, slightly mesmerized by the beauty of the view.

Maddox reached over and held my hand. "Only the best for you."

I settled in and enjoyed the sights.

∾

THE CLOCK HAD JUST STRUCK midnight when we returned. My feet were dying in Vivian's shoes, but the date had been so nice, I soldiered through.

"Thank you for a wonderful evening," he said. We were in his car, parked in front of my house. His car was one of those that automatically shut off when you stopped, so I couldn't tell if he planned to hang out a little or be on his way. I was fine with either, but would've appreciated the clue from the car to help me manage my expectations.

He leaned in close, as if expecting me to meet him halfway for a kiss, but a flashback from *Desperately Seeking Mrs. Right* popped in my head—Joshua kissing me by the pool on the first night at the meet and greet party. Instead of leaning in toward Maddox, I found myself leaning out.

"I'm sorry," he said, eyebrows knit together. "Too soon?"

I nodded. "My neck. Sorry." It wasn't a complete lie. My neck still really hurt. "Besides, I try not to rush into things. That way I have no regrets."

He took my hand and rubbed his thumb over mine. "I would never regret kissing you."

I'm sure he meant what he said, but it was me who didn't want regrets. I'd learned my lesson from Joshua and wasn't going to make the same mistakes twice.

Shaking off the memories, I offered a smile. "I'm sure I wouldn't, either, but it'll give us something to look forward to the next date."

His eyes met mine and it was so quiet I could hear my heartbeat. He leaned in close until I could feel his breath on my earlobe. "I can't wait," he said, his voice soft.

Uh-oh! I think my knees went weak.

After he helped me out of the car and walked me to the porch, I faced him, easily appreciating how attractive he was. His eyes, his lips. I gulped. *Oh, boy, I'm in trouble!* "Thank you for the—" I almost said "best date of my life", but I'd had some pretty amazing dates on the show, "—incredible evening."

"You're worth impressing," he said.

I stepped in the front door, gently clicking the door shut. Someone had left a light on for me.

9

The house was silent; the scent of wassail lingered in the air. I leaned against the door, mentally replaying the scene in the car. I kicked the killer shoes off, which skidded down the hallway and interrupted the perfect silence.

"Elsie?"

I jumped and yelped. "Nana?!" My heart beat a mile a minute. What was she doing there sitting in the dark? "You scared me!"

"Sit down. We need to talk."

My emotions nosedived from elation to concern. *What was wrong?*

I flipped the light switch, which turned on a little lamp with a dim bulb. Nana sat in a rocking chair with both arms on the arm rests. She looked like a mob hitman, lying in wait.

I gingerly sat down on the edge of the couch, wondering what this was all about. "Did you wait up for me?" I asked.

"I waited for everyone to be asleep."

I wasn't following. "Okay?"

"You've gotta bust me out," she said, her head bobbing, as if signaling me to silently understand her meaning.

"From where, Nana?" She made it sound like she meant prison.

"Here. This house."

I leaned forward and whispered, "You don't like it here?"

"I'm a prisoner. I want to live in my own home and do what I want to do."

I scooted over closer to her and put my hand on her knee. "But we're all worried about you living alone. You might fall."

She put her hand over mine. I couldn't help but notice how boney it was and how thin her skin was. "At least I'd die happy."

"You're unhappy?"

"I just want to go home. I like my house and I'm comfortable there. Here, I feel like a fish out of water. And your dad is Mr. Grumpy Pants all the time. Who wants to spend their last days watching political news 24/7 with the volume up to one hundred and constantly hearing ads about reverse mortgages and adult diapers when I could be watching *Golden Girls*?"

She had a point. Dad had been forced into early retirement due to medical reasons two years ago and still grumbled about it on a daily basis. Plus, he was hard of hearing and frequently forgot his hearing aids, so conversations with him tended to be loud. As well as the volume on the TV. My mom had picked up a part-time job at the library just to get out of the house and probably get some peace and quiet. Nana didn't have the option to leave when she wanted.

"I can understand where you're coming from. There's no place like home," I said.

"You get it! Now you're the girl who's going to make it happen."

How? Did she have a plan? Did she have her bags packed already, thinking this escape would happen tonight?

"I'm not sure how to do that," I said.

She patted my hand. "We'll figure that out somehow. Just keep it in mind."

The floor creaked and Vivian peeked around the corner. "I thought I heard someone yell."

"It was Elsie. I'm surprised she didn't wake up the whole house," Nana said.

"You're up?" I asked. Vivian being awake wasn't as shocking as Nana being up

"I can't go to sleep until you tell me about your date!" she said and sat beside me.

"Oh, my gosh! It was crazy! Like my expectations and then—" I made a mind blown charade with my hands. "It kept getting better and better."

"That sounds amazing! Did you kiss?" Vivian asked.

Nana winked. "Inquiring minds want to know."

"No. He wanted to, but I don't want it to be like a Joshua situation."

"Joshua," Vivian said, with vitriol.

"You know, dear, every man isn't going to be a smooth operator like Joshua," Nana said.

I had worked through the feelings and emotions to do with him, but the whole experience left me a little scarred. I no longer threw caution to the wind.

"I know. But my approach to dating is more reserved since Joshua." History would not repeat itself. "The date was so over-the-top, it reminded me of being on the show."

Vivian perched onto the sofa beside me. "Tell me all

about the over-the-top date. Where did you go? What did you do? What did you eat?"

"Well, the 'over' part was an aerial tour of New York City in the helicopter we flew in to get there." I inhaled deeply, because it seemed so unbelievable. "Then we ate at a restaurant at the top of a hotel that had an amazing view of Times Square."

Nana put her hand over her heart. "Oh, my goodness! That sounds lovely!"

Images of flying over the Statue of Liberty came to mind. "It was...breathtaking and exhilarating."

"A guy with that much money wouldn't take you on a boring date," my sister said.

"I was not disappointed." I sighed. "What will I do when it's my turn to plan the date? Watching a movie at home and eating microwave popcorn sounds basic." I bemoaned my fate by flopping back into the Victorian torture couch. My neck made me regret it.

Vivian was not feeding into my dilemma. She smacked my leg. "Quit being so dramatic."

I straightened and brushed her hand aside. "Think about it. Anything I do will be really boring. And I don't want to be boring."

"I guess you'll have to get creative," Vivian said and winked.

"I might need your help with that. I haven't dated seriously since Joshua. Lots of first and second dates, but it never goes any further."

My sister frowned. "Is that because of you or because of them?"

I wanted to shrug, but decided against it. "A mix. Sometimes me, sometimes them, sometimes it's mutual." There were so many ways things didn't work out. The guy wanted to get serious, the guy didn't want to get serious, the guy just wanted to hook up, the guy was boring, he had bad breath… the list went on. Not to mention me. It wasn't always something wrong with the guy, sometimes it was me. The guy was a really nice guy and I freaked out, he wanted to be exclusive and I didn't, he smelled like Joshua, looked like Joshua, acted like Joshua. Any hint of Joshua and I was outta there.

This time, Vivian patted my knee kindly. "Well, I have a good feeling about this guy."

"About him, or his bank account?" I asked, trying to be an adult about this, 'trying' being the operative word. I didn't think I was a totally responsible adult when it came to decisions.

She responded with a silly smile. "Is there a difference?"

Yes, there was. And it was BIG. "Sadly, yes."

"Is he a narcissistic, sexual deviant with sociopathic tendencies, dear?" Nana blurted out.

Nana's inner Betty White shocked me. "Is he what?" I asked after I picked my jaw up off the floor.

"You know, like Christian Grey From *50 Shades of Grey*?" Nana said.

Nana had read *50 Shades of Grey*? Was she leading some sort of double life I knew nothing about?

I cleared my throat. "Not that I know of. I sure hope not. Why would you even think that?" I asked.

"Because Christian Grey was a billionaire. Maddox is a billionaire," my sister said.

"Billionaire does not equate to the same sexual tendencies," I said. "And Nana, I hope it'd be a 'no' to his sexual preferences. Our relationship isn't even at that point yet." Even if it had been, I wasn't going to discuss it with my family. That was my problem with the Fairy Tale Suite on *Desperately Seeking Mrs. Right*. What should've been private, wasn't really private. Instead, it was blasted all over TV and the internet and it left me feeling very exposed. And I hated that. "He was the perfect gentleman and it was a pretty perfect date."

Nana slowly stood and stretched. "Well, dear, I need to call it a night. It sounds like you have a handsome fella that treats you well. Hold on to a man like that."

I was definitely ready to settle down for the night. I had the downstairs bedroom to look forward to now that it was guest-free. It was like the adrenaline from the date ran out and I was about to hit a wall. "Goodnight, Vivian. Goodnight, Nana."

And although she spoke the truth, I wasn't sure if it was my truth.

10

I stared at the blank, poster-sized piece of Stonehenge natural drawing paper on the dining room table, frustrated. I should've been working, but after I'd spread out my materials on the table, I couldn't find a comfortable position. The oak chairs were too hard and the table angle was all wrong.

Nana shuffled in and took a seat. "Who are you killing dear?"

"Killing?"

"Staring daggers with your eyes. I figure you must be mentally killing someone."

"That's what I love about you Nana. Always thinking the best of me." I pointed to my paper on the table. "It's work."

"Are you imagining killing your boss?"

"Who you killing?" Vivian asked, joining us from the kitchen with a cup of coffee in her hand. She set her bulging backpack on the table.

"No one," I grumbled.

"I heard you talking about killing and I thought I should check on you," she said.

"I'm having a hard time working on the flat table."

"Oh, so you and Nana aren't scheming to murder someone," Vivian said.

Was that disappointment I heard in her voice?

"Nothing that exciting, dear," Nana said.

I pointed to Vivian's bag. "Heading off to school?"

She nodded. "Yup. I've got to study at the library. See you later."

We said goodbye and I returned my attention to the table. "Looking down hurts my neck. At home, my desk is adjustable."

"I think Gramps had one of those drafting tables." Nana made a rising action with her forearm, like one half of a draw bridge.

"That's exactly what I need," I said. If I could angle the desk top, maybe I could actually do something.

"It's still at the house. I believe in the blue bedroom." Every bedroom at Nana's was identified by the color of the walls. If we slept over, we always stayed in the "pink bedroom". Nana's was the "yellow bedroom".

I conjured up an image of the "blue bedroom". Gramps had grown up in the Great Depression and saved a lot of stuff, and I think the "blue bedroom" was Nana's solution for managing his clutter.

"It's probably buried under a pile of books or newspapers, but I know it's there. Maybe you want to try working at my house."

I wondered if this was how she was planning on making her "prison break".

She continued. "Look around. I want to know if you think it's unsafe for me to live there alone."

Oh, this was a reconnaissance mission. "Sure, why not?"

It wasn't like I was getting any work done anyway. "I'll go see."

I staggered into the kitchen like a zombie. The keys to Nana's house usually hung on a hook next to the fridge, but they weren't there.

Nana told me where I could find a spare key and I was on my way.

Her small, cedar-shingled house was only about eight minutes away. I had to park on the street two houses up because Nana's PT Cruiser with the fake wood siding still occupied the driveway.

It was sad to see her house like this, the blinds closed, the landscape neglected. It was as if all the life left when she left. I hoped the inside didn't look as depressing as the outside.

Nana said the key would be under the red, plastic pot with the dead plant and gnome in it. I found the pot right where she said it would be at the bottom of the porch steps. The only problem was the spare key wasn't there. Nothing was underneath it except wet ground and some moss. I checked the immediate area, making sure there wasn't some other red pot with a dead plant and fake gnome in it. Did she mean *in* the pot? I dug around the cold, clumpy soil. Dirt was caked under my fingernails when I finally admitted it wasn't there.

Maybe the bulkhead door to the cellar was unlocked. I tramped around to the backyard and gave a hefty tug on the metal handle. I was rewarded with a reverberation sound as the door stayed securely in place.

What the heck?

I tried the windows, rattled the back door, checked under all the dead plants in pots and still nothing.

Behind me, off in the distance, I could hear the wail of a

police siren. Crazy how often I heard that in this tiny town. Sirens were a frequent background noise in Vegas, and I got to the point where I never paid much attention to it.

But it got closer and the wail became louder. I looked around, wondering if something was on fire, but I didn't smell anything burning or see any smoke. Maybe it was an ambulance.

I returned to the front of the house, the siren now deafening. Lights blinked at me as two cop cars skidded up to Nana's.

Oh, no! They're here for me? Did one of the neighbors think I was trying to break in and called and reported me? Adrenaline pricked at my skin and I broke out into a sweat.

Please, please, please don't let it be Officer McCutty! I'd only been in town for three days and I managed to see him every single one of those days. He was going to have the worst opinion of me.

The first officer stepped out of his car, and much to my relief, I didn't recognize him. The second officer got out, his eyebrows up and the look of recognition on his face. Officer McCutty.

"Elsie Lawson, or should I say the infamous Elsie Lawson. We meet again," he said.

I stomped my foot. "Oh, geez. Are you, like, the only cop in this town? Seriously? Or do you have an Elsie radar? Are you personally assigned to me? Is there a BOLO for me? Every time I see you, it's when you're working. Can't I ever run into you when you're not on duty?" Warren was a small town, but come on! This was a crazy number of coincidences.

"Sure. That can be arranged," he said.

Did I just ask him out? That was not my intention.

I stumbled on. "This is my Nana's house," I said, my voice jittery now that I was no longer ranting.

"We got a call someone was trying to break in," Officer McCutty said.

I shook my head rapidly. "I'm not. Really." I pointed to the flower pot. "I'm just trying to find the spare key."

The front door of Nana's house creaked opened.

Wait. What? Someone was in the house?

Vivian emerged, head dropped, cheeks red. "It was you?" she asked softly.

My hands flew in the air. "You called the cops on me? What are you doing in there anyway? You're supposed to be at school!"

Her shoulders sagged. "I heard all this noise outside the house and it freaked me out. I didn't know it was you!"

The other cop spoke into his radio, explaining the situation. My cheeks burned with embarrassment as I listened. I couldn't believe this was happening to me.

"Are you ladies all set then?" Officer McCutty asked, looking between me and Vivian.

I forced a smile. "Yes, I think so. Thank you for your help."

"And your prompt response," Vivian added.

After the cops drove off, I followed Vivian into the house.

I plopped into the over-sized recliner in the living room. "What the heck, Vivian! Why are you even here?"

"I come here to hang out," she said. She perched on the edge of the couch, picking at a hangnail.

"Why?"

"Because I quit school and I don't want Mom and Dad to know!" she blurted out in a gush of words.

I sat up and my jaw dropped. "You what?" How could

she just quit RISD? That had been my dream school. I would've killed to have gotten in there! But she *did*! And she *quit*?! I wanted to grab her shoulders and shake her! How could she give up such an opportunity?

She blinked her eyes and lifted her shoulders as if to say *I don't know*. "I missed a few classes over the summer and fell behind. Then I lost my scholarship because my grades were bad and I couldn't afford to go in the fall. So, I took a semester off. And now it looks like it might be two, because I haven't signed up for winter semester."

"Holy crap, Viv!" We both knew Dad would freak out when she told him. I understood her reluctance.

"I know, I know. I come over here when I'm supposed to be in class. I plan to tell Mom and Dad, but it never seems like a good idea in the moment, so I don't."

"What are you going to do?"

"I don't know. Sometimes it's hard making decisions. I know I have to deal with it, but I'm not ready yet."

I sighed. "Welcome to adulting," I said.

"It's not fun and games," she added, singing the Guns N' Roses tune, *Welcome to the Jungle*.

"It's not everything you thought," I continued.

"Actually, it's quite a pain."

We shared a laugh at our impromptu song.

"Come on," I said, standing. "Help me look around for Gramp's desk. Nana thinks it's buried in the blue room."

"Oh, gosh! Have you seen the blue room? It became a storage room. Good luck," she said.

"Well, since you're here, and you don't have any place to be right now, you can help."

Vivian was right, the room was packed. Boxes, stacks of *National Geographic* magazines, clothes, shoes, blankets, a toaster oven still new in the box, wrapping paper, an artificial Christmas tree with the decorations still on it shoved in the corner. All sorts of random items were piled high on the bed, on the floor, and on the furniture. It made me afraid to peek in the basement or attic if this was what the spare bedroom looked like.

We went to work, moving stuff around (Vivian's responsibility), dragging the Christmas tree into the pink bedroom (also Vivian's responsibility), until we found the desk in question, positioned neatly in the corner opposite where the Christmas tree had been.

There was just one problem. It was big, and really heavy.

"There is no way we're going to drag that back to Mom and Dad's and get it down to the basement. You might just be stuck working here," Vivian said.

It was starting to look that way. "That might not be a bad thing. At least I can escape the noise of Dad's TV."

With a lot of decluttering, some dusting and vacuuming, working in the blue room would be ideal. I just had to wait until my neck gave me the okay.

11

Ding!
The sound of a text woke me up Sunday morning. I rolled over to grab my phone, instantly realizing that I'd forgotten about the literal pain in my neck. The mattress in the downstairs guestroom was much more comfortable than the Victorian Torture Device, but it didn't cure my whiplash.

It was from my roommate, Jade, who was actually now my ex-roommate.

Jade: Remember how I liked how clean Rob's car and apartment always was?

Me: Yes. Nice to not date a slob.

Jade: He's kinda obsessive about it.

She hadn't been a messy roommate. Our apartment was generally in a good, orderly state. Neither she nor I stressed if we left dishes in the sink overnight. As long as they got cleaned up the next day, there wasn't any reason to stress.

Jade: Like really obsessive about it.

Me: Did he freak out about something?

Jade: Yeah. Left a bag of groceries on the table when I

got home from work. Forgot about them. He got home and asked me about them. Then he reminded me that we both had to be responsible for our own stuff. Like I'm not an adult or something.

Me: A big bag?

Jade: Tampons, bag of Hershey kisses and some Diet Coke. Not a big deal.

Me: Doesn't he know not to pick fights when you have PMS?

Jade: Don't know if he figured out the PMS. And it's not that. It was like he reprimanded me.

Me: Sorry. Not fun. You shouldn't feel like you're living with your dad.

Jade: Right?! That's exactly what it felt like! How's living at home?

Me: Going OK. It'll be nice to be home for the holidays (I think).

Jade: Any idea when you're coming back?

I didn't want to remind her I came out here partly because she decided to move in with her boyfriend and told me a month before our lease was up. I tried to talk her out of it—they'd only been dating for two months. Personally, I thought it was a rebound relationship.

I needed a roommate to be able to stay in the apartment. I had followed up on friends of friends who were also looking for an apartment or a roommate. I had even interviewed a few people, but they all seemed a little weird to me. If I wanted a weirdo roommate, I would've advertised on Craigslist. So here I was, forced to do a long-distance search for a roommate, an apartment or both. It wasn't a quick process—it was stressful—because as of December first, I was technically homeless in Vegas. I didn't have much time.

Because my prospects looked so bad there, I had packed up and put my stuff in storage. It was better to be safe than sorry.

Me: Not yet. I was in a car accident, so I'm recovering from that and I'm still hunting for a roommate and/or an apartment.

Jade: What happened? Are you OK?

I didn't feel like rehashing the whole story, especially with her. Honestly, I was a little mad at her for moving out and abandoning me. It had turned everything topsy-turvy and put my life in a tailspin. Her timing had been terrible: just before the lease was up. The kicker? Right before the holidays.

We'd been friends for a couple of years, and in the grand scheme of things, I'd get over her short-sighted decision. But with so much going on, I hadn't dealt with my hurt feelings yet. I had bigger problems to deal with.

Me: Just whiplash. Still recovering. I'll send you updates.

Maybe I would, maybe I wouldn't.

My phone buzzed again. I assumed it was Jade, hoped it Maddox, and found out it was neither of them. It was my boss, Aaron.

Aaron: How's Sweden, France and the Appalachian Trail maps coming along?

Me: I haven't finished them yet.

The reality was I hadn't even started them yet, but I wasn't about to tell him that. No need to stress him out. When he stressed out, I stressed out, and I was already stressed out.

Me: I was in a car accident. Got whiplash. Will keep working on them.

I didn't know when I'd be able to do that, but hopefully sooner than later. I had lost a week packing, moving, and driving across the country. I was going to have to put serious hours in to get them done before the deadline.

Aaron: Feel better.

Me: Thanks!

Aaron: Need them by 12/21.

Me: Already marked in my calendar. Have a great day!

I added the last post to leave things on a positive note. As if I could fool him into not worrying, I could also fool myself. I doubted it would work for me.

12

By Monday, Mom insisted I go to the medical center because the neck pain persisted. Erring on the side of caution, I carefully drove myself there in my brand-new car and got checked out. As suspected, it was whiplash and could be treated with rest, Advil and some prescribed mild muscle relaxers.

I made a beeline for the exit. I looked forward to getting my hand on those mild muscle relaxers.

"Elsie."

In my haste to leave, I almost bumped into Officer McCutty, who was walking out the exit at the same time.

I did a double take. Which hurt my neck. *Again? Seriously? What was he doing here? Did he follow me?*

"Long time, no see" he said, offering a smile.

"Officer McCutty!" I said, flustered.

"Eric."

I stopped, momentarily confused. I stared at him, noticing his deep, blue eyes. "What?"

He blinked. "Call me Eric," he said.

"Eric. Sorry. I didn't recognize you in your clothes."

He squinted, confused.

I slapped my hand over my mouth. "Oh, my gosh! That sounded terrible. I'm sorry! I mean, I didn't recognize you out of uniform. You know—" I stepped off the curb and almost stumbled. He caught my elbow and supported me until I got my footing.

"Dressed in civilian clothes," he said, rescuing me from putting my foot deeper in my mouth.

"Exactly. That's exactly what I meant." I nodded, but stopped immediately. "What are you doing here?"

He held up a large, flat, white envelope. "I had to pick up some x-rays for an old injury for workman's comp. What about you? Were you hurt in the accident?"

I wrapped my hand around my neck. "It hurts to turn my head. It's whiplash, but my mom insisted I get checked out."

"I agree with your mom. Better safe than sorry. Injuries can manifest themselves several days later. You can also be bruised from the airbag deploying."

My ego was bruised more than my body, especially since I kept saying stupid stuff every time I was around him, but my biggest complaint was my neck. "I asked for a neck brace, but I guess they don't do that for cases like mine."

He pointed over his shoulder to the parking lot. "I have one of those travel pillows in the trunk of my car. My sister left it there the last time I picked her up at the airport and has never come to get it. She said I could donate it. Want it?"

"Do you think it would help? I'm willing to try anything at this point."

He shrugged. "Let's go see."

With that, I followed him to his car. Within seconds his trunk was up and he held out a neck pillow. It was a pastel, rainbow unicorn that had the head on one end of the pillow and the tail on the other. The horn poked off to the side because of the way it had been stored in the trunk. Without even trying it on, it was a hard no for me.

"How old is your sister exactly?" My guess was eight, ten, possibly twelve. Or maybe one of those college students who embraced everything unicorn.

"Believe it or not, she's thirty."

I did not believe it, in fact. "I expected you to say twelve."

"Sometimes she acts twelve. She's never been married and goes on cruises twice a year trying to pick up a rich, single man of her dreams."

Curious plan of action. One I hadn't thought of. "And has she?"

"Nope. My parents hope she'll eventually settle down, but she's not quite there yet."

"What does she do that she can afford to travel so much?" Maybe I should give up the poor, starving artist life I'd been living and get a new career.

"She's an insurance agent."

"I have no idea how much an insurance agent makes, but it must be enough to travel."

"It all comes down to priority. She rents an apartment instead of owning a house. I think it'd be more beneficial to pay a mortgage instead of rent, but she says she doesn't want to be tied down. We obviously want different things out of life."

"Sounds like you want stability and she wants to be a free spirit," I said.

"Yup."

There was a slight pause as I struggled to find something else to talk about.

"Want to grab a cup of coffee?" he asked. "I believe you owe me one from the night I pulled you over."

Oh! My gosh! That's right. He remembered! I smiled. "Yup."

He returned the smile. "I know a great place on Main Street where we can also get a sandwich. What do you think?"

My stomach grumbled at the talk of food and I jumped at the chance to spend time with him. "I think I'm hungry. Let's go."

Why hadn't I been this quick to accept Maddox's invitation? Because I needed to get ready, I justified. Besides, this wasn't a date. This was a casual hey-you're-here-I'm-here-let's-grab-something-to-eat situation. This was like hanging out. It didn't feel like so much pressure being around Eric McCutty. He was more in my league, and way less intimidating.

13

We met at *Bagels All the Way* and sat at a small table in the corner by the front window.

The waitress came over for our orders.

"Coffee for me, please," he said.

The waitress looked at me, a second too long. I got that all the time since I'd been on the show. I'd stopped addressing it and learned to gloss over it. It generally worked.

"You don't by chance have Mountain Dew Code Red?" I asked. No one ever did, but it was worth a try.

"No," she said. "We have regular Mountain Dew."

"Regular it is," I said.

The waitress left and Eric turned to me. "Code Red, huh? Is that your favorite drink?"

"Yes. I always ask, but restaurants usually don't have it. But it's worth a shot."

The waitress returned with our drinks and took our food orders.

"How are you enjoying your new car?" Eric asked. He

stirred creamer in his coffee. I was glad he didn't like it black. Rumor had it psychopaths tended to drink their coffee black. Besides, the police department wouldn't hire a psycho, would they? Then the show *Dexter* came to mind. I dismissed the thought. I'd been in Las Vegas too long and met too many crazy men. Hopefully Eric would be a nice, normal guy.

I hesitated. I didn't want to tell him too much about my interactions with Maddox. I sipped on my Mountain Dew, slowly drawing it up the straw to buy some time and wash down the bite I had just taken. The sandwich I had ordered was a chicken salad with apples, grapes and almonds served on a bagel and it was amazing. Only problem was I had to bring the sandwich to my mouth and not my mouth to the sandwich because of my stiff neck. I'm sure I looked ridiculous.

"I feel really blessed. I couldn't afford another car, never mind a brand new one."

"As far as accidents go, I guess you lucked out."

I steered the conversation away from the current topic. "What's it's like policing a small town?"

"I grew up in Bristol, so it's not much different there."

Bristol was the next town over, so he was obviously familiar with Warren. "I'm sure it's totally different than being a cop in Vegas," I said.

His eyebrows went up. "Have you had much experience with the police in Vegas?"

"Nope. I've gotten one ticket since I've had my license and that was for accidently driving the regular speed limit through a school zone."

"Oh, I see, you're one of those."

"One of what?" I faked outrage.

"A nasty school-zone-speeder. One who has no regard

for the sign with the flashing lights or the words: Slow Children Ahead."

"First of all, whoever made the sign 'Slow Children Ahead' came up with that well before political correctness became a thing."

He slowly shook his head, as if completely disgusted. "And yet we still have those up all over town."

"We need to make a campaign. Something more direct. Like 'Slow Down! Kids!'"

"'You! Stop speeding!' With a finger pointing at the driver." He demonstrated by pointing his finger at me.

"We could make it our mission to go around town and correct the politically-incorrect signs."

"I'm a servant of the law. I can't go around breaking it on a crime spree."

"That's a pretty boring crime spree. Please don't plan that for our next date." The next-date-thing slipped out without me even thinking about it. But I was having a good time and definitely hoped we'd have another date.

He flashed a wide smile. "Note to self: plan a crime-free second date."

A second date! Awww!

I swatted at him nonchalantly. "I generally don't make it a habit to break the law. Just so you know."

He pretended to wipe sweat from his forehead. "Phew."

"You won't, like, run a background check on me before we go out, will you? Check if I had any outstanding warrants, unpaid parking tickets or speeding tickets?"

"No, I won't."

I exhaled. "Good."

"Because I already did that."

I stopped chewing and swallowed hard. "When?"

"When I pulled you over for the broken tail light."

"You already knew I was okay to date?" I asked.

"Let's just say you were the best traffic stop I've made."

My smile bubbled up from the inner cockles of my heart. His swoony words my made my insides go mushy. I felt absolutely giddy.

"Now that we've decided on another date, tell me more about yourself," Eric said.

I cleared my throat, trying to take charge of my giddiness. "I grew up here, applied to Rhode Island School of Design, didn't get in, so I moved to Las Vegas with a friend, got an art degree online. All of this is much to my dad's dismay," I said.

He looked confused. "Why? Didn't like the online degree thing?"

I sighed. "He wanted me to be a lawyer." I took another bite.

"And obviously you didn't."

"Nope. I'm more creative than analytical."

"What did you study? What do you do?" he asked, leaning in a little. The tables had filled up while we'd been there, and the chatty atmosphere in the place made it a little hard to hear.

"I studied illustration and now I draw maps."

His eyebrows arched. "Ah, that explains the compass on the accident form. Do you draw road maps? Atlases? Are those even a thing anymore?"

I smiled. "I'll be honest, I've never used an atlas in my life. If my parents didn't have one in the car growing up, I probably would've never seen one before college," I said.

"You don't work for Rand McNally, or whatever the brand was, do you? My parents had one in the backseat of the car. That's what I'd look at on road trips to my grandparent's house." He snorted. "It didn't make the trip any better."

I nodded, familiar with the memory. "Ours was on the floor of the back seat."

He made a stabby motion. "Same! My dad used to lecture me about that too."

We shared a laugh as Eric mimicked some of his dad's lectures. "'*Don't step on the road atlas!*' But he never moved it. It was kind of hard not to step on it, ya know?" It must've been a generational thing, because his dad sounded exactly like my dad.

When I was done laughing, I continued answering his original question. "The maps I make are locations. Countries. Cities. Towns. People order maps of someplace special to them. Clients buy them as gifts for people they don't know what else to buy, or are wealthy and have everything they want already."

"I wonder if I'm like that," he said. "One Christmas my sister bought me a blanket that looked like a giant tortilla."

"Original," I said.

"And warm. I can wrap up like a burrito."

I laughed at his joke. "I've seen them advertised. Secretly, I kind of want one."

"You should get one. Then you could bring it to my house for burrito night. We could eat burritos, and watch *Nacho Libre*," he said, then stopped short.

Our second date sounded like snuggling would be involved. I wasn't opposed to any of it. Not the burritos, the blankets or a Jack Black movie. "Sounds great. When and where? Your place or your place?" I asked, then quickly added, "Since I'm currently living with my family."

But it's just temporary. I reminded myself. *Just through the holidays.*

"I guess it's decided: my place," Eric said.

"Where exactly do you live?"

"On Union Street. A couple of streets from your parents."

Union Street, although close, was a street I'd never really explored and wasn't familiar with.

"Any roommates?"

"It's just me and my dog," he added.

"Ooh, dog. What kind?"

"I have a—"

"Wait, wait! Let me guess. A...pit bull."

"Nope," he said. "Too much of a liability. Especially to insurance companies."

I pictured the police dogs. "A German shepherd."

"Nope."

I smiled. "A Chihuahua."

He shook his head and a smile tugged at the corners of his mouth. "Not even close."

I looked at him closely for a moment, as if I was studying him, and then closed my eyes and conjured up an image. "A labradoodle."

He laughed and shook his head. "Give up?" he asked.

I opened my eyes. "Yes."

"He's a Yorkie."

Huh. Not the big, tough dog I pictured him with.

"Will your dog be at Burrito Night?"

"He'll be there, but will not be allowed to eat any. Mexican food gives him gas and it's lethal."

I hoped the food didn't give *me* lethal gas.

"Do you want to bring the burritos? I'll bring the blanket and stream the movie," he said, then added a wide grin.

I was only an okay cook. My best dish was Oreo cheesecakes, which only called for four ingredients and didn't require any cooking. I'd be searching for a place to purchase dinner from as soon as I got home.

"I guarantee once he smells the food, you'll be his new best friend," Eric said.

"But I can't feed him any."

"Exactly. At all cost, don't feed him any."

He pantomimed dying of asphyxiation. His eyes rolled back in his head, his jaw gaped open and his tongue fell out.

I leaned closer to him. "Is it too much of a gamble?" I asked in a serious whisper.

"You're worth the risk," he said.

I hope I didn't disappoint him. "When should we engage in this risky behavior?"

"How about Wednesday night?" he asked.

My days (and nights) were wide open. "Works for me," I said.

"Tell me your number and I'll text you my address," he said.

I told him and watched as he programmed it into his phone. A few seconds later my phone dinged and his address came up.

"Would six o'clock work?" he asked.

I had to squash the urge to be super smiley. I had a date! Another date! "That works for me," I said.

We finished up, said goodbye and walked to our separate cars. Once I was safely secluded, I let out a *whoop!* I pulled up his text and created his contact as McCutey and assigned "Holding Out for a Hero" by Bonnie Tyler as my ringtone. I drove home, replaying the lunch conversation in my mind.

I wasn't really planning on getting involved with someone for the short time I was home, but it was one date. Just a date, not a commitment or a relationship. So really, what could it hurt? In my mind the answer was nothing. Absolutely nothing. Going on a date didn't mean I was falling in love.

14

When I woke on Tuesday morning, I felt a little better. The combination of the muscle relaxer and Advil alleviated some of the symptoms and my neck didn't hurt as much. I'd gone to Nana's house and cleaned off the desk with the intentions of returning in the afternoon to get some actual work done. On the way home, I'd picked up a bag of catnip treats and threw a few into the bushes in hopes Cowboy the Cat would find them.

"Where did you go?" Mom asked. She was at the kitchen sink, loading the breakfast dishes into the dishwasher.

"Nana's. Gramps has a desk that makes it easier for me to work. I had to clean it up a bit, but it's perfect. I'll probably go back over this afternoon and work."

"I'll come with you," Nana sang out from the family room.

"Morning, Nana," I called out.

She joined us in the kitchen. "When are we going?"

Mom leaned against the counter, facing us. Her brows knit together. "I worry about you falling over there."

Nana motioned toward me. "Elsie will be there."

Mom's lips pursed. "Promise you'll take it easy?" She glanced at her watch. "I'm going in to work at eleven, but Dad's home if anything happens and you need help."

What did she picture Nana doing? Deep cleaning? Climbing ladders? Putting up outside Christmas lights?

Nana beamed. "I promise." She turned to me. "What time should I be ready?"

I hadn't planned a specific time. "After lunch. Maybe about—"

The doorbell rang. Mom was immediately in motion. "I'll get it."

She opened the door and I strained to hear parts of a conversation. It was hard to hear over the TV.

"Elsie," she called. "It's for you."

"Who is it?" Nana asked, voicing the question running through my head.

"I'll let you know," I said. I only came up with two options: Eric or Maddox. I didn't know of anyone else in town, really. I peeked out the window and saw a Tesla parked in front of the house.

Maddox.

He stood in the hallway, his face completely hidden behind lavender roses. It was the hugest bouquet of flowers I'd ever seen outside of a wedding. "These are for you," he said, sticking his head out from behind.

My mouth gaped as I took the roses. *Oh no! They can't be!* "Those are gorgeous!" I exclaimed.

"Just like you," Maddox said.

"And so many." My words flowed out like a flash flood.

There was a low chuckle. "Over the top, right?" He said it like it was a given.

"You don't have to do everything over the top. At least not

for me," I said, and hugged him quickly. I appreciated it, I did. Just too many bad memories from *Desperately Seeking Mrs. Right* came to mind. I knew Maddox was a completely different guy than Joshua, but I couldn't shake the feeling...I didn't actually know. I couldn't pinpoint what my hesitation was.

"That's how I roll."

Take it or leave it, that sounded like how Maddox was.

"I mean, you already gave me a car," I blurted out. "I'm sorry, I mean, wow. I don't want to sound ungrateful. Thank you." The scent of the flowers filled the hallway. "Can you sit for a moment?" I motioned to the horrible sofa. He might sit for a moment, but not stay very long after being on that thing for a few minutes.

I set the vase on the coffee table and I ran my fingers over the silky-softness of the petals until I found the little white envelope poking out from among the blossoms.

Thank you for the enchanting evening. Here's to many more.
—*Maddox.*

I held the envelope up to my heart, then sat beside him and hugged him. I could smell the clean scent of his shampoo. "Thank you. That's so thoughtful."

"I'm glad you like them."

The conversation paused for a moment too long.

Maddox thumbed over his shoulder toward the front door. "You know you have a cat sitting in your bushes? Is he yours?"

I shook my head. "No, but I call him Cowboy the Cat. My family says he's been roaming the neighborhood since this summer."

"You named him and now he's chosen you?"

"I don't know if he's chosen me. I give him a handful of treats when I see him. I don't want him to starve."

Maddox scowled. "It's winter. He's going to need more than that."

"I know, but it's not up to me. I can't bring him in because my sister's allergic to cats."

He glanced out the window, as if assessing the neighborhood. "You're sure he's doesn't belong to anyone?"

I shrugged. "I wish he did. I haven't ever gotten close enough to catch him and bring him to a vet to see if he has a microchip."

"I agree with you that that'd be a good first step."

"But if he doesn't have a microchip, what do I do with him? I can't keep him. I don't want to bring him to the animal shelter. They are always overrun and with Christmas coming, there is always the post-gift surrender. It's sad, really." I followed a few rescue groups on Facebook and saw their posts about surrenders, usually followed up with the encouragement to "adopt, don't shop". "Pets are a commitment. You just never know if the animal is going to be a good fit. It's important everyone gets along."

"It sounds like having kids," he added dryly. "Me and my sister could get into some arguments growing up. And I've seen her kids fight and it's bad. Man. I'm definitely not ready to be a parent."

That was a throwback to my growing-up years. "Do they get into physical fights? My sister and I would get into yelling and maybe hair pulling. But with my brother, Troy, it was different. He was more likely to throw whatever he was holding at me. Broke a couple of windows."

"My sister's kids are calculating. Like the passive-aggressive stuff. Messing with the other's phone, unplugging it when it's charging. Stealing earbuds and hiding them. And the crazy thing is, they do it all the time. At least my brother and I would wrestle and fight and get over it."

"So, it's like the family that pummels together, stays together?" I wondered if our family would've gotten over things quicker with a good wrestling smackdown. At least when it came to my brother.

"Oh, I don't know about that. But...since I don't have kids to worry about, I can at least worry about this cat. Should I buy him a little cat house?"

"My dad would love it if you got him out of the garden. Maybe something we could put by the fence." I pointed to the opposite side of the yard.

Maddox nodded. "Okay. And I'll buy him some food." His alarm went off again. He glared at it, then silenced it. "At least we'll know if he's eating."

His show of concern was touching—he was possibly an animal lover, or at the least an animal liker. "Great," I said. "But he's still kind of cautious about approaching humans. I usually throw the treats on the porch, shut the door, and watch from the window to make sure he eats them."

His phone pinged and he glanced at the screen. "Actually, my meeting got pushed back and I have some time right now. Want to go shopping?"

"Now?"

"Sure. Let's go to the pet store and see if we can find some things that will change his mind."

I glanced at my watch. Technically, I wasn't planning on working until after lunch. I had a few hours to spare. "Yes," I said.

With a quick Google search, we jumped into his car and with a low hum, we were off.

15

We stood in the entrance of the pet store, both with shopping carts, at Maddox's insistence. "What do you think we need?" he asked.

Having never had a cat, I didn't know anything beyond the basics. "A litter box, but he's an outdoor cat, so maybe not. Food, and possibly one of those tall cat perch things. But again, he's an outdoor cat."

Maddox pulled his phone out of his pocket. "This site provides a list. I'm sending it to you now. I only have an hour before my meeting, so let's divide and conquer. You take the top half, I'll take the bottom half, and we'll meet back here in fifteen minutes. Let's see who fills their cart first."

His enthusiasm was contagious. I went left, he went right. My phone dinged with his text, and I checked out my assignment: cat toys, food and water bowl, food, snacks, and a scratching post. I debated about the scratching post, because, again, he was an outside cat. Couldn't he just scratch a tree?

After the allotted time, I met Maddox at the designated

If the Ring Fits

spot. He was on the phone and I could hear bits of the conversation.

"I got it. I know the date. I'll be there."

He made eye contact with me as I approached.

"I'll be ready. Hey, I gotta go," he said and immediately ended his call and put his phone away.

I examined his cart. It was overflowing with boxes and things. Had Maddox had cleared out the cat section? My cart had two toys, two bowls, cat food and snacks.

He lifted up a box with an igloo pictured on front. "Hey, hey! Check this out!" He then proceeded to unload his cart, one item at a time, holding it up and showing me. I felt a little like I was watching Home Shopping Network. He went through a cat sling, cat backpack, soft pack carrying case, hard carrying case, a tree condo, an activity center, toys (on top of the ones I got), a cat bed, a cat hammock, a harness and a leash.

"A leash? Do you really think the cat will need a leash?" I asked.

He examined the packaging and description on the leash. "Dogs do. Why would they have cat leashes if cats didn't use them?"

Because people like him had extra money to spend on extra things that the cat probably wouldn't use.

"And maybe wait on the tree condo until you have him, don't you think? How are you going to fit it all in your car?"

He quickly lifted the box out of his cart and set it near an endcap. "Good point."

"What do you plan to do with all this stuff?" I asked.

He looked at me like the answer was a given. "Use it."

I playfully elbowed him. "I know that, but don't you need the cat first?"

"Sure. But I figure if we buy him this stuff, get him used

to us, then we can trap him and get him checked for a chip. If he doesn't have a chip, I'll bring him home with me and I'll be all ready for him."

It warmed my heart that Maddox wanted to take responsibility for Cowboy the Cat.

Maddox continued. "He's had a really rough life, I think, being abandoned, and I want him to have a better life."

The cat had a better future living arrangement than I did.

∽

BACK AT MY parent's house, we unloaded some of the stuff we thought I'd need until we were able to trap Cowboy the Cat and move him to Maddox's.

We set up the igloo in the front bushes at the corner of the porch, where he normally hung out. I stepped back to admire our handiwork. "This should—"

Maddox's phone dinged, buzzed and lighted up. He looked down, studying it. "Sorry," he said. He typed out a response that was answered immediately with another ping. He glanced up at me, then thumbed toward the car. "I *really* need to go."

He leaned in a little. Was he going in for a kiss? Should I meet him halfway? Was he going to cover the rest of the distance?

His phone dinged again, which distracted me. The three seconds it took me to analyze and not make a decision allowed the moment to pass. He moved away a miniscule amount, but enough that I felt awkward going in for a kiss when he just pulled away.

Should I address it? Last time I over-analyzed. A mere

five seconds ago and I lost my chance. "Thanks." I stepped in and gave him a hug.

His arms wrapped around me and he hugged me back. I breathed in his scent of aftershave and took in his warmth.

"Talk soon," he whispered in my ear. His breath tickled my skin. His phone pinged three more times. Someone really needed to talk with him.

"Looking forward to it!" My farewell was enthusiastic as was the wave I sent him off with as he drove away.

Attractive, sexy and an animal lover! Oh, boy! What's not to like?

I waved him off before adding the bed and blanket in the igloo, a bowl of water next to it and a small serving of cat food. I probably should've stayed out there to see if Cowboy the Cat appeared, but it was too cold. I'd check on him later.

16

Back inside, Nana and Vivian were sitting on the Victorian torture contraption, admiring my roses.

"Mr. Billionaire is trying to impress you," Vivian said.

"He's trying to win your heart," Nana added.

Vivian held up the card and her hand went to her heart. "That sounds so romantic. I'm jealous."

"I don't get it," I said. "I would've thought taking me out fulfilled any sense of obligation he felt. And he's done that."

"Maybe he's attracted to you dear," Nana said.

"Maybe," I said. "I honestly thought it was a one and done. And now Officer McCutty."

Vivian grabbed my knee and squeezed. "Wait! What?"

"Oh, yeah. I have a date with Officer McCutty," I said.

"McCutey too?" Vivian yelled. "You're in town for four days and you're already dating two guys."

"Only one date each. Second dates haven't happened yet, and, who knows? One of them might change their mind and cancel." I continued working to sound calm, but it wasn't without effort.

"What do you call buying all that cat stuff together?" Nana asked. "That's a date in my book."

I nodded in agreement. "True."

Vivian pulled an exaggerated expression of curiosity. "So, which one are you leaning toward?"

It was a little bewildering. A huge smile finally broke through. "I don't know. I need to spend time with both of them to even know if I want to date them. I don't know enough about either of them, yet."

"I already know enough about Maddox," Vivian said.

"Really?" I was curious how she came to that conclusion so easily.

She scooted forward. "Think of the trips, the food, the shopping. It all sounds so magical," she said wistfully.

"But what if he has all that money and is the most boring person in the whole world?"

Vivian quirked her eyebrow. "Was he boring on your date?"

"No. But the first couple of dates is when everyone is on their best behavior. Trying to show all of their good qualities." There wasn't room for much conversation in the helicopter. It was loud and hard to hear.

"You don't think money makes a guy more attractive?"

"Yes and no. Lots of money seems to equate an easy life, but does it guarantee it? I don't know. But not having to worry about money is definitely something I'd love to have in my life." Sometimes I was a literal starving artist. And right now, I was like a lean artist. I was just making enough to get by with a little extra left at the end of the paycheck. I'd love to have a little more financial security.

"I think the balance in the bank account would make my decision," Vivian said.

"Don't you want to marry for love?" I asked. I know I did.

I learned with Joshua, a whirlwind romance did not equate to love, no matter how I added it up.

"I would be in love. With him and his money," she said.

I threw a pillow at her. "You aren't that shallow."

She shrugged. "It's kind of hard to see past all those zeros following the dollar sign for his net worth."

"As much as I love visiting with you guys, I need to head over to Nana's and get some work done."

Nana stood. "I'll grab my coat!"

I sighed, thinking of the enormity of my tasks.

"I won't disturb you, will I?" Nana asked.

"Of course not!" I said. Even if she would, it was her house and I'd never tell her that. "But I won't be able to hang out. I have maps to draw, an apartment or roommate to find, and life details to be dealt with."

"Why do you need to search for an apartment, dear?" Nana asked.

Dang it! I was trying to keep myself from letting that slip. "Because my roommate met a guy, moved out last month with only a month left on the lease. I didn't renew it because I couldn't afford the whole rent myself."

"Could you find another roommate?" Vivian asked.

"I wish I could've before I left. Believe me, I tried. But finding a normal roommate in Vegas is really hard, especially if you don't know the person beforehand. The apartments I can afford on my own are in really sketchy parts of town where you don't dare go out alone at night."

"Why didn't you tell me, Elsie?" Nana asked. "I might've been able to help."

Despite the offer, there was no way I was going to ask my Nana, who lived on a fixed income, for help with my rent. "Thanks, Nana. I totally know I could've asked you."

"But you didn't," Nana said.

"I thought I had it worked out, and had a roommate, but they flaked and now I'm stuck and missed the window to renew."

Nana clapped her hands so loud I jumped.

"By George! I think I've got it!" Nana said.

"Got what?" I asked.

"A solution, of course."

Vivian leaned forward. I waited.

"I can be your new roommate and we can live in my house!"

She looked at me expectantly, as if I'd immediately answer "yes". Which I wanted to. I mean, it solved a number of problems: a place for me to live with the perfect desk and Nana would be back at her house. It sounded like a win-win to me.

"I'm going to agree with the understanding that my return-to-Vegas date is to be determined."

Nana hopped up and hugged me. "Bring it in, Roomie!"

17

The next day was my date with Eric. Because he lived so close to my parents, I decided to walk to his house. I found a restaurant that had good reviews and ordered some burritos and Spanish rice for takeout. I packed it up in my mom's insulated casserole dish and carrier so it wouldn't get cold. I also had a little "doggie bag" with a *puppy patty* treat for his dog. The closer I got to his house, the heavier the food got. I regretted not having the food delivered to his house.

His house wasn't what I pictured. In my mind, I conjured a hunting lodge—log cabin design with those post walls, natural wood tones in a glossy seal coat, a moose head on the wall, a ten-foot-tall taxidermy black bear in the corner, and a large, stone fireplace in the center. And a pool table.

He actually lived in a small split-level house. You know the ones where you walk in the front door to a landing, and you can either go upstairs to the kitchen/living room/dining room/bedrooms, or downstairs to a family room. There was a one-car garage nestled underneath the second story where I assumed the bedrooms were located. There was nothing fancy about it, nothing creepy about it, just a basic, boring house that blended in with the other basic, boring houses in the neighborhood.

I shifted the food carrier strap in the crook of my left arm and tugged at my jacket—really Vivian's, which was a tad too small —with my right. The waistline kept creeping up around my rib cage. I rang the doorbell and waited. I counted the visible puffs of air as I waited to hear footsteps from inside.

When he opened the door, my breath hitched. Was it possible to like his look even more out of uniform? He was in jeans and a plaid, flannel button-down, but he wore it well. He extended his arms wide. "Welcome to Casa de McCutty."

I stepped in. "Thank you," I said.

He took the food from me, which I was grateful for. My arm was killing me.

The TV was on upstairs, but was quickly drowned out by the yapping dog that came racing down the hall and confronted us at the top of the stairs. It was a mop of a dog with long, golden hair.

"This is Giant," Eric said.

Giant was definitely not a giant. I knew he was a Yorkie, but with a name like Giant, one might expect a little more size to him. He looked about five pounds, but his attitude was not limited to his size. Despite the plastic cone on his neck, he still barked and growled at me like he thought he was a large, ferocious guard dog.

"Giant!" Eric warned as he went up the stairs, past the dog, and set the insulated food carrier on the table. What he lacked in size, he made up in attitude.

I followed behind cautiously.

Giant growled at me, showing his teeth. Eric scooped

him up. "Giant really is the sweetest dog once he knows you're supposed to be here."

"If he doesn't know, what does he do? Take me out at the ankles?" I laughed at my own joke.

Eric covered the dog's ears. "Sshh. Don't let him hear you. We've really worked hard on his self-esteem. He doesn't want to accept that he is a little guy."

Did I risk reaching out to the little guy at the chance of losing a finger? "How long does it take for him to warm up?" I asked. Did he bring a lot of women home? Did Giant act like this because he was constantly invaded by a parade of women coming in and out of Eric's life?

"Give him like five minutes. If you pass his test, he'll be your best friend."

"What's his test?" I was genuinely curious.

"I'm not sure, but the girlfriends Giant didn't like never lasted very long."

How many girlfriends had he had?

"So Giant is like the litmus test for girls you date, but the dog version?"

"Pretty much, yeah. He peed on one girl. That was embarrassing. Another one he chewed a hole in her shoe."

I made a mental note to keep my shoes on.

I held up the doggie bag. "I brought him a treat." I handed it to Eric.

He peeked inside the bag and nodded. "Oh, he'll definitely like you." He put the dog down, unwrapped the treat and handed it to him. Giant gobbled it up in a few bites.

I smiled. Winning the dog's approval was important to me. "Have you had a lot of girlfriends?" It slipped out, before I had a chance to think about it or quash the impulse.

I immediately regretted asking the question because we

were literally on our first official date and barely in his front door.

He shrugged it off and motioned me to sit down on the couch with him. "Ah, two or three. Two serious. One in college and one about three years ago. How about you?"

I didn't want to discuss me at the moment. I wanted to discuss his two or three girlfriends and the two serious ones. How long were the relationships? Why did they break up? Were these the same girls Giant didn't like? Would Giant like me? What if he didn't? Did his opinion—or bark—really matter in this case? So. Many. Questions.

"Me, well," I cleared my throat, "like you, I've had two. Maybe one and two halves." I didn't really know how to classify Joshua. I thought we were "serious" enough that he was going to propose to me at the end of the show. In fact, I was sure of it. So sure, I spent the night with him in the Fairy Tale Suite. We'd had a "connection".

"One and two halves? How does that work? Did one, like, die, before you were done with the relationship?" He pulled an exaggerated, confused expression.

I carefully shook my head. "The first one was in high school. You know, high school sweethearts. I just knew that we were going to get married as soon as we graduated college. Then he went to Boston University to play football and got a girl pregnant the first semester."

Eric cringed. "Ouch. And this was all while he was still dating you?"

I scratched at my neck. Was I a hypocrite? I was currently dating two guys. I pushed the thought in the back of my mind. No, I wasn't in a committed relationship right now. This was different. "Yup. I was a senior in high school. Needless to say, he did not take me to Homecoming that year."

"And the next one? The half boyfriend?"

I decided to skip over Joshua. I didn't want to ruin the mood with talk of him. "No one important. Dated him for a really short time."

He cocked his head. "And the last half boyfriend?"

Ugh. Another sticking point. I didn't want to think or talk about Maddox while I was with Eric. "I wouldn't really consider him a boyfriend. Just a couple of dates." I pointed to the burritos. "We should eat before these get cold."

He nodded and we went about setting the table and dishing up the food. We sat down and ate. Luckily, the conversation flowed freely.

"This was amazing. So good," he said. His table was a round, tiny pub-style table, close enough to make everything about dinner feel intimate. "I could've kept eating if we didn't eat it all." He offered me a smile and ran his hand over his five o'clock shadow.

I scraped the plate with my fork and licked the tiny amount of sauce that collected. I had my elbows perched on his table. "Small confession," I said, then stalled.

He held my gaze as he waited. "Okay."

"I didn't cook dinner. I'm a horrible cook. This is takeout." To emphasize my shame, I shaded my eyes with my hand.

He pointed an accusatory fork at me. "That sounds like three confessions to me."

I blushed. "I guess."

With a little clank, he rested my fork and knife in the center of the dish. "It was delicious," he said. "I don't care if it was takeout. Takeout's great. I generally burn everything. So why take the chance, when I can order out instead?"

"Right?" I agreed.

"I thought that sauce tasted an awful lot like Miguel's. Is that where you got it from?"

"Yes," I said, then cleared my throat. This was a little bit harder. "I have another confession."

His eyebrows went up. "Another? Let's hear it."

I fiddled with the napkin in my lap. "I've been on a few dates recently, but he's not my boyfriend."

"Is this the half boyfriend?"

I shrugged. "It's not exclusive. I just want to be open with you. Let you know I'm dating other people."

He seemed confused. "Okay."

I suppressed the urge to keep talking and going deeper into an explanation of the dating situation that I fully didn't have a grasp on. I moved on to a topic I was more comfortable with. "Is it movie time?"

"Yes."

With that, we cleared and rinsed the dishes before settling on his couch. Giant jumped up next to me and curled up in a ball. It was a small reassurance that I might possibly have his lick of approval.

Sure enough, Eric pulled out the tortilla blanket. In order for us to share it, we had to get in close to each other. There were no complaints from me about that. We chanted "Nachooo!" at the fight scenes, died laughing at the party scene where Ignacio had to sing, and cringed with second-hand embarrassment about his "expensive" clothes. Once the movie was over, we joked about our favorite parts.

But the best part was being snuggled up to Eric.

At the end of the night, Eric held my hand as he walked me home. The moon shone bright against the cloudless sky and the air was still cold, but my insides were all warm and fuzzy.

18

My phone dinged, waking me up. It felt like my life had turned into *Groundhog Day*, but instead of being woken up by my alarm, I was woken up by a text notification. What time was it? I felt around for my phone and forced my eyes open. I swiped on my phone to see what time it was. The glow from the phone screen was so bright against the dark morning, I squinted to see it. Friday, Dec. 3, 6:42 am. It was a good thing the phone reminded me of the date, because all the days sort of blurred together when I had no set schedule.

Maddox: Can I come see Cowboy?

Why was he up so early? And texting me? I was barely awake. Actually, I was still asleep.

I wiped the sleep from my eyes, sat up and turned a light on. I hoped this wasn't going to become a habit of Maddox's, because I'd have to nip it in the bud. It was far too early to be coherent.

Me: I don't know if he's even here, silly!

Did I want to encourage him to come over? If he did, I'd

have to drag myself out of bed, get dressed, deal with my morning hair and morning breath.

Maddox: You could check.

Me: Then I'd have to get out of bed.

Maddox: You're still in bed? I've been up for hours.

Was he one of those morning people that wake up at four a.m. and assumed everyone else was up?

Me: My work day starts later than yours. I don't feel guilty one bit.

Maddox: So, I can come over?

Me: When?

Hopefully later. Like really later. Like afternoon-later.

Maddox: Does now work?

Um, not very well, no. But I could make it work. If I hurried.

Me: Drive slow. I need a few minutes.

Things were always a rush with him. I rolled out of bed, frantic. I stripped off my pajamas, flinging them by the arm and kicking them off, and digging around to find something to wear. This rushing routine was getting old, fast. I found my jeans scrunched up under my sweats. Those would do. I pulled on the sweater draped over the back of a chair.

I dragged a brush through my hair. There was a flat spot on the side of my head that wouldn't go away no matter how many times I brushed it. That wouldn't do. With a few twists, my hair became a messy bun. I looked in the mirror and saw there was a crease running down my face, temple to cheek. It was from the sheets, which I always, inevitably, wrapped around my wrist and across my face. What could I say? I liked to snuggle under the covers. I brushed my teeth (just in case kissing would be involved) and was ready to go.

Racing up the stairs two at a time definitely got my

blood flowing. I shoved my bare feet into my boots and sat on the arm of a chair by the window waiting for his arrival.

Did I look desperate?

Probably.

Was I excited?

Yes. Maybe more like looking forward to seeing him. It wasn't bad for him to know that.

"Whatcha waiting for?" Vivian asked.

She surprised me, coming up behind me. I almost lost my balance and fell off my perch. "What are you doing up so early?"

She pointed to her name tag pinned to her shirt. "Work. What's your excuse?"

"Maddox is coming over," I said.

Her face broke into a wide smile. "You like him."

She said it more as an observation than a question; her voice had a pleased tone to it.

I nodded. "Yes. I enjoy spending time with him. He has a big heart when it comes to Cowboy the Cat."

"Are you falling for him?

Ding. My phone lit up.

McCutey: Are you free Sunday night?

Why was he up so early? Was everyone in this town always up this early? Despite my unanswered questions, I couldn't ignore the shiver of excitement that ran through me.

Me: Yes.

McCutey: Want to grab dinner or something?

Me: Yes! What time?

McCutey: 6?

Me: Yes. See you then.

I looked up from my screen to see Vivian watching me.

"That your Maddox?" Vivian asked.

I shook my head and set my phone down beside me. "Actually, it was Eric McCutty. We're having dinner Sunday."

She bumped me with her elbow. "Nice."

It *was* nice. But complicated. Dating two guys? How long could I keep this up? And two "dates" in one weekend? That was just plain stupid.

Maddox's freaky quiet car rolled up and parked by the sidewalk. I pulled on a puffer coat hanging by the door. "Wanna come see Cowboy the Cat?" I asked her.

She scowled. "No! I don't want to be a third wheel."

"This isn't a date," I said. Because, in my mind, I had quotation marks around date. That meant it was being loosely defined as a date.

"Does he know that?" she asked.

I considered it. Every interaction wasn't necessarily a date. Besides, this visit was about the cat.

I opened the front door to a blanket of frosty air. Man, I missed the mild, barely-could-be-considered-winter winters of Las Vegas. I breathed in and the cold went right into my lungs, causing me to cough. Coughing caused my eyes to water, which then sent tears rolled down my face and stung my cheeks. I'm sure that really added to my already-super-cute morning look I was rocking.

Maddox's super cute morning look was actually super cute. He wore sweats and a thick hoodie; his curls were tamed and his face freshly shaven.

"You okay?" he asked as he stepped on the porch.

"Yes," I said, still trying to clear my throat.

"Do you need me to pound on your back?"

I shook my head. "I'm fine now."

He quickly kissed me at the edge of my lips/border of my cheek. "Good morning," he said. It was such a fast, fluid motion, it surprised me and I didn't have a chance to respond. I think I tasted a small hint of Chapstick.

"Hi." I smoothed my hair and tried to regain my composure. I think if it wasn't so cold outside, I would've turned into a puddle of goo. Although, I would've liked to have had a better kiss. That one didn't quite do it for me.

Maddox peered into the bushes to where the cat igloo now loomed, taking up half the garden.

"Is he there? Can you see him?" I asked, twisting to see for myself.

He held the rail for support. "I don't know," Maddox said. He squatted so low I thought he'd fall over. As he stood up, some of his curls fell into his eyes. He brushed them back, then looked directly at me and caught me watching him.

The slow smile he gave me was nothing short of beautiful. Embarrassed, I quickly looked away.

When I was brave enough to venture another glance at him, he was still watching me. "Should we knock on the igloo door or just set treats outside and hope he'll know it's for him when he wakes?" he asked.

Speaking from recent experience, I knew I hated being woken up. "Let's set out the treats and leave Cowboy the Cat alone. I'll check back later to see if he ate them." Hopefully, it wouldn't attract any ants, rats, or other unwanted pests.

I retrieved the bag of meaty morsels just inside the front door. Maddox and I spread out a few around the entrance to the igloo and some a little farther out. "Now let's see if that tempts him," I said.

"Want to grab some breakfast while we wait?" Maddox asked.

I was so *not* ready to go anywhere, but I agreed anyway. I

motioned for him to follow me in the house. "Sure. But I need to put socks on."

I need to put socks on? I just admitted that to him? It conjured up a pair of stinky, sweaty feet. My brain was not awake yet. Who knew what other dumb things I'd say this morning? I put myself on notice.

I tried to recover. "Come on in for a minute."

"Okay."

He smiled and my insides turned to jelly.

Oh, my goodness. I grabbed the rail and steadied myself.

19

As soon as we stepped into the warmth of the house, I shut the door quickly.

I rubbed my hands together and stomped my feet, trying to shake off the numbing cold that had set in. I stepped on one heel of my boot, then the other, and stepped out of them, careful to not step in the little puddles that had formed on the oak floors from the melting snow.

"My socks are downstairs. I'll be right back." As I ran down the basement stairs, I realized I should've invited him in, like farther in than just the front hall. Even the Victorian Torture Device was better than just leaving him standing there.

I rifled through the clean laundry in the basket on top of the dryer, figuring I'd find a pair of socks faster that way than searching through my suitcase. I grabbed the first pair that would do, pulled them on, and took the steps two at a time as I raced back up to where Maddox waited.

"Okay," I said, trying to catch my breath. "I'm ready."

He pointed to my feet. "Don't forget your boots."

"Right." That would've been embarrassing.

He leaned in close, squinting. "And I think your sweater is on backwards."

I looked down, squishing my chin to get a look. Sure enough, I pulled away the neck band and there was the little J. Crew tag. Now that was embarrassing. I pulled my arms out and tried to right it and still maintain my dignity. I don't know if I succeeded. "Okay, now I'm really ready."

We walked to his car, his hand on my elbow. I assumed it was there just in case I slipped. I appreciated the gesture.

He started the car, blasting the heat. The air made the hair on his forehead blow straight up. "Any suggestion for breakfast? I'm still new in town and haven't scouted out all the good places yet."

"I know a place uptown. Only problem is the parking. We might have to park two blocks over and then walk."

"I can walk."

I appreciated his attitude. I hated the inconvenience, especially since it was a cold morning. "Parking is a big deal in this town. I'm not used to it. In Vegas, most businesses have their own parking. Downtown and the Strip have parking garages. Everything is made for convenience there. Here, not so much."

"Yeah," he said.

I directed him down the narrow streets to the restaurant. "It's not a fancy restaurant, but the food is good." It was the one I'd gone to with Eric. "It also has plenty of seating and not just a couple of cramped tables." Cramped tables didn't encourage lingering.

"Pretty much any place will do if you're in good company."

A bubble of happiness filled my stomach. "I couldn't agree more."

"Parking is tight," he said, scanning both sides of the

street. It took a few minutes, but he was finally able to find something. Although it didn't leave us without a short walk.

"It's one of the downfalls with old towns. They were established before cars were a thing," I said.

We found a small table in front of the window and the waitress poured us some coffee and took our order almost immediately.

I added some sugar and cream to my coffee and stirred it in. I anticipated the warmth that the first sip would bring. "Speaking of small towns, how are your plans coming along? Is everything working out?"

He took a sip of coffee. "Not really. I'm struggling with permits. Some neighbors are against having a business this size in their neighborhood—the pushback is unexpected. And the traffic it will cause is also a hot topic of debate."

"I imagine it is."

"But I'm persistent and I think it'll work out in the end." He followed up his statement with a smile. His beautiful smile.

"What if it doesn't?" I asked. I watched out the glass-front window as all the cars slowly inched forward, getting no place fast. I returned my attention back to him, studying his expression. "Meaning the town doesn't agree to all your requests? Or it's not worth the time and energy to put into it? Sometimes some of the laws or codes are either archaic or just ridiculous or just for the purpose of money-grabbing."

"There's always a contingency plan."

A waitress brought my strawberry and crème crepe to me. I thanked her and tried a bite. It was everything the description in the menu promised.

He spread some cream cheese on his bagel. "In this case, there's several other viable options. I'm really hoping this one works out. I think I like it here." His eyes met mine.

"Not everything is a sure thing."

He held my gaze and gave me a small smile. "True. But I have a good feeling about this thing."

I half-expected him to wink. Was he talking about us or his business? I still wasn't sure.

"Good feelings don't always guarantee it's going to work out how you want it."

"Sounds like you have a story behind that reasoning."

"I do."

He waited for a moment. "What is it?"

I stirred my coffee and took a sip, buying time. I'd gone so long not talking about the show. I had no idea how he'd react when I shared my past. "That dating show I was on? The one I mentioned in the helicopter? That was just six months ago."

His eyes widened. "Really?" The screen on his smart phone lit up. He glanced at it, swiped it, then returned his attention to me. Then his smart watch lit up. He ignored it also. "Sorry. You were saying?"

"At first it was amazing. All the glitz and glam, the group dates, the single dates, the places we got to see and stay at. Joshua was a dream guy—attractive, charming, fun. It seemed too good to be true."

"Was it?"

"Very much so." My mind flitted back through some memories. I quickly pushed them aside. "I made it down to the final three women. We did the hometown visit, met my family, pretending like this was what life would be like if we were married."

He tilted his head. "Did he propose? That's the endgame of those shows, right?"

I nodded. "Exactly." I took a sip. "Thing is, he didn't propose. We made it to the actual proposal, and he broke up with me right then. He told me it wasn't me; it was him. Original, huh? That he wasn't in love with me, it was all a mirage. It was humiliating and devastating. I really thought he would pick me. My rejection was televised nationwide. My stupidity is in syndication."

"You're being too hard on yourself."

Maybe. Maybe not. "I'm trying to leave the past in the past."

"I can help with that. Let's do something fun today. Let's go skiing."

I thought of my neck, my lack of ski clothes, how little time I'd have to prepare. "I'd love to, but I need to recover from the whiplash first."

"Next time, then," he said. "How about hanging out in Newport today instead?"

Him saying hanging out pulled like a hang nail. Maybe now was a good time to clarify things. "Are we just hanging out or dating?"

"We're definitely dating."

I took a deep breath. "For the sake of transparency, I want to be upfront about my dating stance. I'm dating other people and I'm not looking for anything serious or long-term. Besides, I'm only in town for a couple of weeks."

"What you're saying is I have competition?"

He didn't sound like he was asking a question. It was almost a statement.

"No. Yes. I don't know. I don't want you to feel like that."

"It's only natural for a man to feel like he needs to step up his game when he finds out there's competition."

I pictured him puffing his chest, perhaps even beating it with his fists. And competition. Yuck. It reminded me of that awful, conniving attitude that pervaded the house on the set of *Desperately Seeking Mrs. Right*. Dating shouldn't be a competition.

"Look, I appreciate your intentions, but I'm really trying to keep things casual, get to know you, enjoy the time we spend together."

"What if I want more?"

Good question. What if he did?

I cleared my throat. "Let's not put the cart before the horse. It's going to be a problem if we get serious and then I move back to Vegas."

"Why is that a problem? I can visit. I could buy a house out there. I don't see any roadblock that would be insurmountable."

An itchy, scratchy, uncomfortable-in-my-skin sense came over me. Why was he in such a rush? I hated rushing. Everything was rushed on the show and look where it got me. "Whoa, there, Maddox. Let's slow things down. You might not even like me after date number three." I tried to make it sound like a joke, but I failed miserably. I had the sudden urge to ask for the bill and escape.

"It's not every day that I meet a beautiful woman I'm interested in. When I want something, I go after it one hundred percent."

I was finding that out.

My love life flashed before me, like a skier on a double black diamond slope, when I knew I should only be on the bunny hill.

I reached over and put my hand on his. "Let's just take our time and not make any rash decisions." If there was one thing I learned on *Desperately Seeking Mrs. Right*, it was that.

20

In an effort to concentrate on work and block out any distractions, I forced myself to shut my phone completely off while drawing. After a drawing sprint, or marathon, my reward was turning my phone on and checking my messages and social media. Sometimes, it was a power nap on the newly-cleared bed. So far, it seemed to be working.

As my phone fired up, the dings came in and I stood, stretched, grabbed another Code Red Mountain Dew (both for hydration and stimulation, of course) and relaxed for a few minutes and answered messages.

Jade: Got a promotion at work.

Me: Cool! New position?

Jade: Shift lead.

Me: Congrats! Raise?

Jade: Yes. $1/hour more.

Me: Very cool. Don't spend it all in one place.

Jade: I know. Any news on when you're coming back? I miss you!

Me: How's the boyfriend?

Jade: Things have been good. As long as I pick up, he's generally happy.

Me: Good. Happy for you.

Jade: How about you? What have you been up to?

Dating two guys.

That was an upside to breaking up our roommate relationship. Mainly, I came home and met two great guys. But then the downside was I met two great guys.

Me: Still on the hunt for a roommate. Know anyone? LOL!

Jade: I'll keep asking around.

Me: Thanks!

I had been hunting around for a new roommate. I had checked Facebook, 4you2, Nextdoor—even Craigslist—all the apps I could think of. I joined ISO (In Search Of) roommate groups, but so far had only received a few replies. The most interesting one had come in this morning.

Random Number: You texted about renting a room?

Full sentence, correct grammar. So far, so good.

Me: Yes.

Random Number: I'm Joe

Me: Hi Joe. I can't remember which listing you were. I've sent info requests for a bunch today.

Joe: 3 bedroom house. You'd be renting the 3rd bedroom, shared bathroom

Me: Is the other roommate a guy or a girl.

Joe: Girl

That made me feel a little safer.

Me: Where are you located again?

Joe: Sunrise Mountain

That was way in the Northeast, away from where I had been living.

Joe: We're open here

What exactly did he mean by that?

Me: You mean you still have an opening?

Joe: Open floor plan, open 2 relationships, open relationships, whatever u open to

Oops, his grammar just took a nosedive as did my interest.

I promptly blocked his number and shut my phone off while I tried to shake the "ick" vibe I got from his texts. I hoped he was going to be the exception and not the norm for my search.

21

Sunday night, Eric and I had a date. He picked me up at six o'clock in front of my parent's house. I wore Vivian's coat again because he'd told me to wear something warm. A light dusting of snow covered the ground, and by the gray color of the sky, more would come.

He smiled and our gaze met when I got in his truck. His lingered until I felt myself blushing.

I dropped my eyes. "What?" I asked, finally, breaking the slightly uncomfortable silence.

"You look beautiful," he said.

Heat crept up my neck and cheeks. "Thank you. You're looking pretty attractive yourself. I like what you got going on here." I gestured rubbing my jawline.

He mimicked my action. "I'm glad you don't have this going on with you."

I shook my head, my hair brushing across my shoulders. "You wouldn't love me if I was the bearded lady?" I halted; my words hung in the air. Did I just say the "L" word, even if it was in jest? Instead of looking at his face and searching his expression, I cleared my throat. "I mean like. Would you still like me—"

"I like you now. Just the way you are."

I leaned close, across the small expanse of the cab. "And just so you know, I don't have a beard."

He wiped imaginary sweat from his forehead. "You had me worried, for like a second, that secretly you were the bearded lady. Good to know."

I was glad I'd shared all my confessions last date and didn't have any other deep secrets I needed to unload. "No need to worry about that."

He pulled a Code Red Mountain Dew from his console compartment. "I got this for you, just in case you were thirsty."

"Ooh, thanks! I appreciate it." I wasted no time cracking it open and taking a sip.

"Feel like going Christmas tree shopping?" he asked.

"Sure. Do you go to Home Depot?"

His expression was one of mock horror. "Home Depot? Is that where you buy your tree?"

I pictured the tree I had in Vegas. It'd seen better days, but I couldn't afford to replace it. Yet. "Depends on what you're in the market for. You might get a better price on a fake one at Hobby Lobby."

"Fake one?" he choked out. "What are you talking about? We don't do fake here. It's real or nothing. I'm talking tree farm, cut down the tree, drag it through the woods, to the car, tie it on top."

I imagined the whole scene, but then *National Lampoon's Christmas Vacation* popped into my head. Anything like that would be a disaster. "You're talking the whole experience."

"The whole experience, baby."

Did he mean to call me baby? Or was it part of the playful banter we'd been sharing?

"Would we really have to trek out and find the tree and chop it down ourselves?" I hadn't worn my winter boots.

"We could."

I looked down at my sneakers. "I'm not wearing the best shoes for that."

"We'll look at the precut ones, then. I'm sure we can pick out the perfect tree."

"You trust my opinion?" I teased.

He grabbed my hand and squeezed it. "I know you'll make a good choice."

With that, we drove to the tree farm. It was located in a more rural area of town, landmarked by the bright lights and Christmas music being piped through speakers. There was something magical about the strings of lights lighting up the perimeter, reflecting off the snow, walking through a maze of trees, holding hands. I forgot how cold it was and enjoyed the moment.

"Pencil or full?" I asked. I guessed he'd go for full.

"Definitely full. I always buy the same type of tree. A blue spruce. I like the way it looks, like the way it smells. What about you? Do you have a preference?"

"Honestly, Hobby Lobby."

"You're really team Fake Tree? I can't believe it." He said it with a note of fake disappointment.

I shrugged. "I sort of inherited it from a roommate who moved out and left it. It was just easier."

"So, convenience over quality?"

"Yes, when it comes to trees."

We looked at a series of trees before coming upon the "one": it was not too thin, but not too full; not too short, but not too tall. "I think that's perfect," he said.

I stepped back and placed my hand on my hip, assessing it from afar. "It looks nice."

He carried the tree up to the cashier and paid. I helped him (kind of) load the tree onto the top of his SUV, but it was mostly holding the bungee cords while he secured it to his roof rack.

He blasted the heat once we were in the car driving home. We drove in silence for a few minutes. The snow had started up again, and the roads were narrow with no shoulder, so I was okay with Eric paying attention to the road and not to the conversation.

"You know, you never told me about the other 'half' boyfriend. The one you barely dated."

I scratched at my wool cap. It was so itchy. Why did I choose that one?

"The other was when I was on a reality dating show, *Desperately Seeking Mrs. Right*, and I was one of the final three girls to choose from."

Eric glanced at me. "Meaning what? Like he'd choose you to be his girlfriend? I don't watch reality dating shows."

We'd only been on a couple of dates, and usually this early in a relationship I didn't go into details. But with Eric, it felt safe. "So, the basic premise of the show is you take twenty-five attractive, available women and match them all with one attractive bachelor. Each person matched seems to be matched to his likings, whether it's looks, emotional intelligence, extra-curricular activities, and so on. Some are just a wild card, I think, or just there to cause drama."

"Okay."

"He spends time in group dates and one-on-one dates, systematically filtering out the girls he doesn't like, doesn't feel like are a good fit, or whatever other reason he comes up with. It's a brutal and vulnerable process for everyone, but especially for those who don't get selected to stay."

"I bet," he said.

"Anyway, long story short, I made it down to the final three. We did meet-the-family dates, and had the opportunity, after, to spend the night together in the Fairy Tale Suite. At first, because of the situation, with it being on TV and knowing he could possibly sleep with the other two girls, I decided not to do it. He begged me—convinced me—that we should. He said it was 'the only way to take our relationship to the next level'. So, I did.

"I'll admit, on some level, I wanted to. I had so many hesitations, but I wanted him to pick me. I thought sleeping with him would cement his decision. I thought everything he said, he really meant. Then he didn't propose."

"Did he promise he would propose?"

I nodded. "In the Fairy Tale Suite. They don't film or record anything, for obvious reasons, and he told me I was the one."

Eric took my hand in his. "But you weren't."

I grimaced. "Nope. I was so humiliated. Especially because my family, my dad, especially, would watch the show and know what I did. So, I kneed him in the crotch and walked off the show."

"What?!" Eric slammed on the brakes at an approaching stop sign. "You seriously did that?"

"Yes."

"No way! Nice move!"

The street light reflected on his face as he smiled. It was like my mind took a photograph of the perfect moment. We were at his house within minutes.

"Let's get this fella off the roof before we go inside."

It seemed easier to unload the tree than to load it, and

we had it propped up in a corner by the front porch with minimal effort.

"Why don't you bring it inside right now? I could help you," I said.

"I didn't think ahead and make room for it. Once I move things around, then I'll bring it in and decorate it."

I whipped off the wool cap as soon as I was inside in his warm house and scratched my head all over. Feeling freed from the itchy wool, I peeled off my coat and sat in the living room. Eric prepared two cups of hot chocolate before we settled on the sectional, Giant on my lap (the final lick of approval?) and I finished my story.

"There was some backlash for my behavior, talk of being charged with assault. Honestly, I didn't plan to react that way. It was literally a knee-jerk reaction to the jerk."

He stretched his arm across the back of the sofa and his fingertips barely brushed my shoulder. "You weren't charged, though?"

Of course, as a cop, he'd be interested in that.

"Luckily, no. I had to issue a formal apology and jump through some other hoops, and show up for the event finale, but once I was done with that, I distanced myself from the show. No reunion shows, no alumni shows, no *Hook-Up Island*."

He twisted a lock of my hair around his index finger. "Do you regret it?"

"Which part?"

"Any? All?"

I shifted my position on the couch. Immediately after the experience, I'd get emotional about the situation. Then mad. First at Joshua, then at myself. "It was a hard life lesson. I made mistakes, but I acknowledged them and moved on." Hopefully I had learned from it and wouldn't ever repeat it. "In the end, Joshua wasn't who I belonged with."

He leaned in. "You're right." His eyes flicked to my lips. "You haven't found your Mr. Right yet."

"Nope," I murmured.

"Let's see if we can change that," he whispered softly in my ear before finding my lips.

As his lips touched mine, I closed my eyes and gave into the moment. *Had I really learned my lesson?* Because at this moment, I might've been failing. Or falling.

22

After a few minutes of cuddling, Eric pointed to the kitchen where some utensils were lined up on the counter. "Ready to make up some dessert?"

I stood. "Yes. Just remember, I'm a horrible cook," I said, still teasing. "Consider yourself warned."

He raised his eyebrows. "Are you really that bad?"

"Sometimes I burn things."

"Hopefully not tonight." He handed me an apron. It was white, scratchy and stiff. "Alright, then, let's get cooking," he said. He pulled on a matching apron. The fold lines were still visible.

I held it up for inspection. "Did you buy these for tonight?" I asked, a smile breaking across my face. He was so cute, buying matching aprons. I guess since they were both plain, it was hard *not* to match.

He offered a helpless grin. "I didn't want you to think I'm a complete caveman."

I leaned in close, catching a whiff of his aftershave. It was light, barely there, but enough to be something. A smell I associated with him. "Can I tell you a secret?"

He got closer. "Yes."

"When I cook," I said in a low voice, "I don't always wear an apron."

"Can I tell you a secret?" he whispered back.

"Yes," I said, inches from his face.

Was he going to kiss me again?

"Sometimes, when I cook, I only wear an apron," he said.

I pulled back, caught off guard by the image of man legs poking out of an apron. "Really?"

He chuckled. "No, not really! Can you imagine what that'd be like frying bacon? Ow! Ow! Ow!"

"Phew." I made a show of wiping pretend sweat off my forehead. "You had me worried for a second. I didn't even want to ask what you do when you barbeque." I hoped to get the chance to barbeque with him.

The thought hit me by surprise. That would mean I'd still be here in the summer, which wasn't in my original plans.

He ran his fingers down the seam of the apron. "I'd think by the fact these are both brand new, that'd give me away. I don't cook very often. I do grill, but that's usually burgers, dogs and chicken. But this," he motioned to the packets of food arranged neatly on the counter—a dessert kit from those home delivery companies, "isn't how I normally eat. It's just easier to actually make a meal when everything is all ready to go. Hope you like apple crisp."

"I don't care if it's delivery, takeout, in a box or frozen," I said.

"Fast and easy is how I tend to go."

"As long as that doesn't apply to how you like your girls," I said.

"Ha ha. Maybe in high school that was every boy's dream, but not now. I've grown up."

"Good to know."

We chopped, mixed and crumbled our way to a delicious-smelling dessert, all the while talking and joking. He told me his plans to become a detective, home improvement projects he wanted to start, what he did in his free time. I told him my aspirations of someday having my own freelance illustration company where I'd make enough to support myself, my Vegas housing/roommate dilemma, among other things. The conversation flowed easily and comfortably.

"Cooking is much more fun when we're cooking together."

"I obviously cook better when I'm with you since I haven't burned anything yet," I said. Maybe it was the oversight, having him watching the food to make sure it didn't burn.

After I put the apple crisp in the oven, the conversation continued and time slipped away. "Baking is definitely much better when you're around." He reached out to take my hand.

He made it sound like everything was better when I was around. It was a nice compliment. "I feel the same way," I said.

"Want to know something else?" His voice was back to that soft, low level.

I found myself drawn to him with each word. "Yes."

"I like you." I could feel his breath on my face.

"I like you," I murmured, inches away from his lips. It was more than just enjoying spending time with him.

He pulled back suddenly. "Do you smell smoke?" His eyes widened.

I sniffed the air. Smoke! "The apple crisp!" As I jumped up, knocking over my chair, I looked over my shoulder and could see wisps of smoke curling along the ceiling.

DANT! DANT! DANT!

The smoke detector pierced the air with its ear-splitting warning.

DANT! DANT! DANT!

Eric got to the oven before I did; smoke billowed out the door. He flung it open, which released more smoke.

I instinctively opened a window, and cold air rushed in as the smoke escaped outside. Eric had a dish towel in hand and waved it at the smoke detector in the living room. I looked under the sink and found the fire extinguisher and stood poised to use it if I saw any flames.

When the annoying blare of the alarm ceased, we looked at the carnage to assess the damage. Our apple crisp was burned to a crisp.

I put the extinguisher back in its place and slumped into his embrace "I forgot to set the timer."

He wrapped his arms around me, his hands resting on the small of my back and kissed my forehead. "It's okay. I still have the vanilla ice cream that was supposed to go with it. You like vanilla ice cream, right?"

I stepped back. As I pulled away, our eyes met and within milliseconds, his lips found mine. I relaxed, kissing him back. I liked the feel of his touch and the security of his arms around me. My insides felt all warm and fuzzy.

Who needed dessert when he was so sweet?

I let myself be lost in the moment and by the time he walked me home, hand in hand, I couldn't deny I was falling just a little for Eric McCutty.

23

The next day I was back at work, pulling my head from the clouds and trying to concentrate on work. My date with Eric had been so swoon-worthy, I found my thoughts floating back to him. I forced myself to concentrate and shut my phone off completely so I wouldn't be tempted to text him.

After what felt like a marathon, I took a break. I turned my phone back on as I set down my pencil in the well at the bottom of the desk. I stretched my back, my wrists, my neck and silently cursed the Appalachian Trail for having so many mountain ranges. It made for more work on the map. The dings came in as I went to the fridge to grab another soda, stepping over the two empty bottles of Code Red Mountain Dew on the floor. I'd gather them all up later.

I went into the living room, where Nana was asleep on the couch, *Golden Girls* still playing on the TV. She had come over with me that day to "keep me company".

I fell into a recliner, enjoying the softness of the seat after spending hours with my butt "glued" to a desk chair.

Jade: Any luck?

I didn't know why she was so interested. Maybe she was curious because we were friends and didn't realize I was grumpy with her.

Me: No. The market is crazy. Competition fierce!

Jade: I can see if my cousin can help. She answers phones at a real estate office.

I didn't want to tell her I didn't hold much hope in her cousin helping me out. It'd be different if she was an actual real estate agent. Or even better, a leasing agent at an apartment complex. But she wasn't.

I wished she hadn't moved out and we had just renewed our lease.

Me: Any help with apartments, or even a roommate, is appreciated! I seem to be a magnetic for the weirdos!

Jade: Like sicko weirdos?

Me: Check this one out from yesterday.

I forwarded her the messages of the following conversation:

Me: I'm interested in the room for rent in the condo
Her: It's available
Me: Great. Move in 1/1?
Her: Yes. I'm vegan
Me: OK, I think you mentioned that in the ad
Her: It's a vegan kitchen
Me: What does that mean?
Her: No animal products
Me: Like I can't eat them? Or can't have them in the kitchen?
Her: No animal products in the kitchen
Me: Cooking or at all?

I could understand and respect her diet and beliefs. If she didn't eat meat, she might hate the smell of meat being cooked in the kitchen.

Her: At all

What was I supposed to do? Have a mini fridge, microwave and an Easy Bake Oven in my room? Maybe eventually upgrade to an air fryer when I could afford one?

Me: *Thanks for your time, but I like to have an occasional hamburger and it doesn't sound like it would work out.*

Jade: Sounds like she'd be uptight. Like my guy, just he's not vegan.

Me: Hey, I've gotta go. I have 3 maps to do before Christmas and I'm way behind.

Jade: Ok. Good luck!

The next set of texts were from Maddox:

Maddox: How are you?

Me: Been working straight for the last few hours. Taking a break and then getting back to work.

Maddox: Want me to help you take your mind off of things for a while?

Me: Would love to, but honestly can't. My deadline is fast approaching. Would love to take a raincheck, though.

Maddox: Deal.

And last, but not least, were Eric's texts, checking up on me.

McCutey: How are the maps coming?

Me: Not as fast as I'd like. I'm sick of the Appalachian Trail.

McCutey: Would some trail mix help or hurt the situation?

His creativity and sensitivity made me smile.

Me: Help. Definitely help. Although I can't visit.

McCutey: Maybe you'll have time to go out on the weekend?

Me: I'd love to! Obviously, I have my priorities straight.

McCutey: Saturday? I have a great idea.

Me: What?

McCutey: It's a surprise. A tasty one.
Me: Yum!!
McCutey: I'll do a trail mix drive-by and text you to let you know. I won't disturb you.

Forty minutes later I found trail mix and Code Red Mountain Dew left at the doorstep.

∽

THE NEXT TWO days I buried myself in work, stopping only to eat, drink and sleep. I'd check my phone, but not take the time to respond to texts as I was in a manic push to finish the first map.

Finally, at 12:13 a.m. on Wednesday, I collapsed on the bed in the blue room, exhausted, un-showered, but accomplished. I had conquered the Appalachian Trail.

24

After dragging myself back to real life, I packaged and shipped the map to Aaron, went home to my parents to let them know I was still alive, and took a long, gloriously hot shower. Maddox and I made arrangements for him to come over and pick up Cowboy the Cat, who seemed to have moved into the igloo while I was working.

The sun shone bright as I opened the front door and stepped onto the front porch. I took a moment to bask in the light, having felt like I'd been living under a rock for the last few days. There had been a light snowfall the night before of about an inch, which was quickly melting. Water dripped steadily off the roofline and the ground had damp patches where the snow had dissolved.

Maddox had just parked in front of the house when I came out. He walked up to the steps but didn't go any farther, probably to avoid getting wet.

He cracked his knuckles and pushed up the sleeves on his jogging suit jacket. "Are you ready to do this?"

"You act like we're going to rumble," I said.

He jogged in place, warming up for the main event, I

guessed. "Just excited. This is a big step in my life, getting a cat."

"I'm excited for Cowboy the Cat to go to a good home. You're going to be an excellent cat dad."

Maddox investigated the area around the igloo, ducking and weaving to avoid the defrosted snow run-off. "Is he in there?"

I nodded. "Usually if I put out some treats, he'll come out. Sometimes he comes over to me and rubs himself against my legs. I've even managed to pet him a time or two."

"He's used to you. That's good."

I held up a baggie. "I got treats."

I handed him some and I took a few and we made a trail from the door of the igloo to the bottom step of the porch. "Now we wait." I sat on the bench safely away from the roofline.

Maddox sat beside me. "We probably need the crate or a carrying bag, right?"

"I'm way ahead of you," I said and motioned to the supplies I had lined up against the railing. It was almost everything we had bought on the shopping spree. Not knowing how this would go or what we would need, I figured it was better to be over-prepared than under-prepared.

"How long does it usually take for him to come out?"

"That depends on the day. Sometimes it's immediately and sometimes it's longer than I want to hang around for."

"What do you think? Grab him as soon as he comes out or let him eat some treats and come to us?"

"He'll probably be in a better mood if he snacks first. It might help him trust us."

"Good, good," Maddox said.

After a few minutes, he poked his black and white spotted head out. A few more minutes, and he emerged.

As soon as Cowboy the Cat was fully out, Maddox pounced and grabbed him with both hands.

What is he doing? That's not what we planned.

"Quick! Grab the carrier!"

I wasn't ready for his spontaneous ambush and it took me a second to spring into action. I grab the soft-sided carrier and stumbled down the stairs, shaking the bag open.

Cowboy the Cat was literally splayed in the air, his hair on end, all four legs spread, claws out.

Oh, boy!

"Hurry!" Maddox cried, trying to wield the unruly cat in my direction.

I scrambled to get the zipper undone. It was stiff or stuck or something, because it didn't move.

"Meeeeeeeoooooooowwwww!"

Cowboy the Cat screeched bloody murder as I finally got the zipper to move. "Here, here!" I rushed to Maddox's side, holding the flap of the bag open.

Maddox tried to get Cowboy the Cat in, but he was not having it. His paws pushed the bag away and he arched his back so much he curled into a ball and his back claws got Maddox.

"Yeeeeeeeoooooooowwww!" Maddox yelped, releasing the cat.

Cowboy the Cat, freed from Maddox's grasp, landed on his feet, and sprang under the porch.

Maddox examined his hand, which now had two bloody scratch marks on top of it. "That didn't go as planned."

I shouldn't have laughed, but the way he said it, you could tell he was surprised. As if he somehow really thought suddenly snatching a cat around the ribs and shoving it into a bag was going to work.

With some effort, I stifled my giggles. "I'm sorry. Do you want me to get you a Band-Aid or something?"

Maddox shook his head. "I'll live."

I bent down, looking under the porch. Cowboy the Cat crouched like he was on high alert, ready to run at the slightest hint of movement.

"Maybe we can catch him if we put the bag over him, scoop him up and zip it really quickly," Maddox suggested.

It sounded like something you'd see on a madcap cartoon. "I don't think that will work," I said.

"No?" he asked, sounding perplexed.

"No."

"We should at least give it a try."

"Cowboy the Cat is going to be completely traumatized by the end of this."

Maddox looked at me earnestly. "How else will we catch him?"

"I don't know. I've never owned a cat."

"Let's do it. If it doesn't work, maybe we'll look it up on YouTube or something."

Maddox got down on all fours, despite the damp ground, and ducked his head under the porch. "Here, Cowboy. Nice kitty."

"Heeeeeeeeeee!" Cowboy the Cat hissed.

"Doesn't sound like he's going for it," I said.

Maddox stood up and brushed himself off, but had dark circles at his knees. "Do you think you can lure him out with treats and I'll be ready with the bag?"

"I can try," I said, but was very doubtful. I retrieved the bag of treats and squatted back down, making eye contact with the cat. I threw a few treats in his direction, but he didn't make a move. I sighed. This could take a while.

Instead of continuing the staring competition, I laid out another trail of treats leading out from underneath the house. "Maybe if we act like we're ignoring him, he'll be fooled into coming out." I didn't have a whole lot of faith in my plan, but it was the only idea I could come up with.

After a few minutes, much to my surprise, the cat appeared.

Maddox made a grab for the bag. "Now!" he yelled, dropping onto his knees. Cowboy the Cat zig-zagged out of the way and took off running.

I pointed toward the backyard. "He went that way!"

Maddox, determined to give chase, jumped up, but slipped and skidded, going down on one knee and ruining his expensive pants. Without hesitation, he was back on his feet, running after the cat.

I debated what I should do. Go around the opposite side of the house, meet Maddox in the middle and hopefully catch the cat? Wait to see if Maddox called for me? Go anyways to check on him? I didn't know what was the best course of action.

Before I had a chance to make a decision, Maddox returned from the direction he had gone. "There has got to be an easier way," he said, wiping a dirty hand across his forehead. His jogging pants were not only stained now, but the knee had ripped and there was a smear mark across the thigh where Maddox had wiped his muddy hand.

Maddox sunk down on the bench, and his head hung low. He was out of breath and panting.

I put my hand on his shoulder. "Somehow, I don't think chasing the cat is going to work."

His elbows rested on his knees and I could see a fresh rip in his pants, probably when he slipped. "I give up."

"There's got to be something we can do," I said and pulled my phone out.

Maddox looked up at the same time and his eyes widened in horror. "You didn't film that did you?"

I wished I had! It was hilarious. "If I posted your video of Maddox vs. Cowboy the Cat, you would've gotten a million views. I shouldn't say it, but it was hilarious."

"But you didn't, right?" He waited for the answer, his body rigid.

"No. I wouldn't do that to you."

His body relaxed visibly. "Thank you," he said, still panting.

I didn't have any ideas on how to proceed, so I swiped my phone. "It's time we turn to the experts: Google."

He also pulled out his phone. He scrolled through a few articles, watched a few videos, then finally looked up. "I guess we'll try putting some food in the crate to lure him in, then wait."

"Do we need to pretend we're not interested or just not be around for a while?" I asked.

"Who knows? Let's open one of those packets of food, put it in the igloo and when he goes in, we'll grab him."

I didn't have a lot of faith in Maddox's plan, but I didn't exactly have any bright ideas myself.

Maddox dug through the purchased supplies and pulled out a packet of wet food with broth, peeled back the silver seal and placed it in the igloo. He had to get down on his hands and knees to manage the feat, but in the end, he was successful.

"Now we wait."

But for how long?

Our wait lasted no more than five minutes before it was interrupted by Maddox's phone. Of course. I was surprised it took this long to ring.

"Excuse me," he said, putting his phone to his ear and walking toward his car. He was still within hearing distance, so I didn't think I was eavesdropping on the parts of the conversation I heard.

"Hey. Stop stressing," he said. Then he made chopping motions with his hand. "No, I don't want to talk to her. No! No—hey, how are you?" His voice went from commanding to fakely sweet.

Curious, I turned so it looked like I was watching for Cowboy the Cat, but really, I was trying to hear better.

He let out an audible sigh. "I know, I know. There's no need to freak out—"

He took a few steps to me, covered the mouth piece, pointed to his car and whispered, "I've got to take care of this, so I'm going to go. I'll call you later."

I nodded. I really needed to get some work done. As soon as Maddox left, I planned to head to Nana's. I'd work for a couple of hours, then come back and check on Cowboy the Cat. Right now, I had to go face the country of Sweden.

25

I stepped inside my parents' house to grab my purse and my keys. The warmth of inside enveloped me as I rubbed my hands together and shivered. It really was cold outside even though the sun was out and the snow was melting. And it was definitely too cold to continue cat-trapping shenanigans. We might have to try it again when the weather was warmer—like in April.

Everyone was home, but the house was strangely quiet. The TV wasn't blaring at its normal volume and there were no voices chattering in the background. Where was everyone?

It didn't take too much sleuthing to find my family, who were all sitting stiffly in the family room. Dad was in his recliner, Mom in the armchair and Vivian and Nana on the couch. Vivian pulled at a hangnail, Mom crossed then uncrossed her legs, and Nana and Dad were silent.

"Did I miss the memo of a family meeting?" I asked, stopping before I crossed the imaginary threshold into the room.

"Did you know your sister quit school?" Dad said, anger lacing his words.

I clucked my tongue. "Oh, we're having *that* discussion," I said, then went and sat between Vivian and Nana. This was definitely something I'd want to sit down for. "Yes, I found out since I've been here."

"And you didn't say anything?" Dad said.

I lifted a shoulder. "To who? You or her? It's kind of a done deal and we can't really do much about it now."

Mom leaned forward, resting her elbow on the arm of the chair. "We're just surprised. That's all."

"And Nana wants to move back to her house," Dad said, throwing his hand in the air.

I couldn't decipher what Dad was more upset about: Vivian and Nana's confessions, or not being in the loop enough to know what was going on.

"Dad, I understand you're upset I didn't tell you about school, and I'm sorry. It just sort of happened and snowballed into what it is now."

"We want the best for both of you," Mom said, looking from Vivian to Nana. "We want you to be educated and you to be safe."

"I would like to live at my house, at least while Elsie is home," Nana said.

"Elsie is just visiting," Dad said gruffly.

I was not about to chime in about my homeless in Vegas situation, so I kept my mouth shut. And Nana wasn't going to reveal all she knew because that was the key; I was here indefinitely.

"I don't think that's an unreasonable request," my mom said.

"I'd be there with her, so she wouldn't be living alone," I chimed in. "She already hangs out there while I'm working.

Now we can both be there and you can have your house back."

Out of the corner of my eye, I could see Dad's shoulders relax, a sure sign of compliance. He sighed. "Do you think while you're here you can convince your sister to go back to school?"

"Only Vivian can convince Vivian to go back to school," I said. I had enough things on my plate. I wasn't going to take on someone else's responsibility.

Vivian gave me a private smile as a thank you.

Nana clapped her hands and stood up. "Let's get moving!"

I looked past Nana to my mom and saw a sadness pass over her face. I wondered if having Nana there was a buffer between her and Dad's grumpy demeanor. Maybe it wasn't just Nana's safety that was the root of having her there. Maybe my mom liked the company. Maybe that was something that would eventually be sorted out. But now was not the time.

∼

My packing involved shoving whatever clothes I brought with me back into my Vera Bradley bag. Nana's packing was a little more complicated, with making sure we had all her meds, shower bench, slippers and such. While Nana packed with the help of Mom and Vivian, I checked my messages. There was one from Aaron checking on my progress, one from Eric, three from Maddox and one from a number I didn't recognize. I dealt with Aaron first.

Me: Started on Sweden.

Aaron: Great. Work some magic because we need those maps delivered by Christmas.

I would've like to have said it'd take a Christmas miracle for that to happen, but really, it would take long hours and hard work.

I smiled as I read Eric's text.

McCutey: Want to go out tonight?

Me: Can't. Moving to Nana's today.

I thought of what that would mean in terms of having her live in the house.

Me: Probably have to take her grocery shopping too.

McCutey: How about tomorrow night?

Me: Yes, I'd love to.

I shouldn't have said yes. I didn't have time to date. I had to find a roommate, a place to live and get two more maps done. But I couldn't help it, I really liked Eric.

Me: I'm working on the map of Sweden and will need a break by tomorrow night.

McCutey: Need Swedish fish?

Me: Yes! Love Swedish fish!

Maddox had sent me a picture of him after the cat trapping incident.

Maddox: Cowboy-1, Maddox-0

Me: Maybe it's time to hire a professional?

Maddox: I'm not giving up yet.

Me: OK. I'll let you know the next time I see him.

Cowboy the Cat sightings would be less now that I was moving in to Nana's, but that might have to be something I dealt with once the maps were done. I really didn't have time to stress about things out of my control right now.

The last text was from a girl named Sage.

Sage: Hi, are you still looking for a roommate? Me too. I'm 25 and have a job.

Me: Hi Sage. Yes, still looking. Looking to start renting in Jan. or Feb.

Sage: My lease ends in January. Feb. would be perfect.

Me: Where do you work?

Sage: Library district.

That sounded like a good, steady job.

Me: Non-smoking? Vaping?

That was in the ad, but I always double-checked.

Sage: No to both. How do you feel about pets?

That had also been in the ad, but it didn't hurt to reiterate.

Me: I'm pet friendly. What do you have?

Sage: I'm a cat person.

I thought of Cowboy.

Me: I don't mind cats, as long as you clean up after them.

What must've been a glimmer of hope started to grow.

Me: Could you send me your info and some references please?

Sage: Sure. Give me a few minutes.

She seemed like she could be a nice person. Maybe a phone call was in order.

Me: It might be a day or two before I get back to you. I have a huge work deadline I'm up against.

Sage: Ok.

A few minutes later, my phone dinged. I checked it to see if Sage had sent her references.

Sage: Would it be okay if you sign the lease and I just pay you the rent?

Me: Why?

While I waited to hear back from her, I checked out her online presence. From her 4you2 profile, she looked pretty normal. Although when I searched her photos, it looked like she had more than one cat. More like five cats. I cringed. That was a lot. Probably more than I could deal with.

Her reply came while I was still going through her photos.

Sage: My credit score is low.

Red flags popped up all over the place.

Me: How low?

Sage: I filed for bankruptcy two years ago.

I give up!

Me: Sorry, I'm not comfortable with that. Good luck with your search.

I made the decision to stop searching for a place to live now and deal with it later. After the maps. After Christmas. After New Year's. It was just too much to deal with right now. I had to focus on what was important: getting these maps done before the deadline. The only thing I would take breaks for was food, bathroom and men.

I wasn't completely freaking out yet about my living situation because I could push my return to Las Vegas back a little, thanks to Nana. Besides, I was dating a couple of great guys. And it felt like I could possibly have a future with one of them.

∼

MUCH TO MY SURPRISE, Cowboy the Cat was sitting on the top step of the porch when I opened the front door. He stared at me and didn't run away. I wondered if he sensed I was leaving. I set my bag down on the bench and retrieved the bag of treats I kept on the table by the front door.

I held one out, to see if he would come to me. He didn't move. I placed a handful on the decking, then sat beside my bag and watched. What would he do?

In another surprise move, he ate the treats. Then he came and rubbed himself against the bottom of my legs. I carefully reached down to let him sniff my hand before scratching between his ears. Why the sudden show of affection? Maybe he was ready for the next step in our relationship?

I patted my knee to see if he would jump up. He did! While I rubbed his head, he ran his body across my lap, arching his back in happiness. Or what I assumed was happiness.

It was now or never. I carefully picked him up, securing him in my arms.

"I'm ready," Nana said, practically dancing out of the house. She held two reusable grocery bags, one in each hand, and was bundled up in her winter coat and pink hat with a glittery pom pom on top. She stopped short. "You caught the cat?"

"He came to me."

"Is he coming with us?" Nana asked.

"Maddox wants him. Guess I'll let him know."

For fear of not being able to catch Cowboy the Cat again, I didn't let go of him until we were in the car with the doors closed. Surprisingly, he didn't leave my lap.

I texted Maddox, who wasn't able to drop everything and come get Cowboy the Cat. He did make arrangements for Wilson to meet me at Nana's and transfer ownership. Nana was happy to be back home, but Cowboy the Cat didn't seem too sure about going with Wilson to his new home.

26

All day Saturday, I attempted to conquer Sweden—that is, the map of Sweden. I popped Swedish fish and guzzled Code Red, which I quickly learned not to do immediately after one or the other, because it created a taste akin to paint thinner.

Around four o'clock, I stopped. I needed to shower and get ready for my date with Eric. It was the best way to end my otherwise tedious day.

He picked me up at five, and we drove together to our yummy surprise.

"It's not Jell-O wrestling, is it?" I asked.

He laughed. "No. I like to eat my food, not play with it."

"You don't have to blindfold me to keep the secret a little longer, do you?"

"Sorry," he said. "No blindfold. I hadn't even considered it. That could cross the line into suggestive things, so it's probably better that I steer clear of it." He smiled as if he was amused with himself.

"Probably so," I agreed.

When the Bank of America Tower, dubbed Providence's

Superman Building, appeared as we travelled on I-195 west, I got more and more excited. After a few turns, we pulled up at Johnson and Wales, a local award-winning college that specialized in hospitality.

"Are we going to their student-run restaurant?" I asked.

He chuckled. "Actually, we're going back to school."

"What exactly does that mean?"

He glanced at me, catching my reaction. "We're going to a cooking class," he said.

"What?" my mouth dropped open. "That's awesome! I love that!"

His face lit up with enthusiasm. "We need all the help we can get," he said. "It's a beginner's class, so we're starting with the basics."

The image of our burned dessert popped into my head. "Right?" It was quickly replaced with another image, a better image, of a white plate with food neatly arranged on it, topped with a drizzle of some sort of sauce. I didn't know what my imaginary dinner was, but it was delicious. I had high hopes for the evening.

The class came complete with aprons and chef hats. I instantly felt more skilled just dressing the part. Eric and I were placed at a cooking station, like something you'd see on those cooking shows on TV.

Chef Michael, our instructor, explained about basic cooking equipment and menu planning, proper food-handling skills and knife skills, including vegetable chopping and paring. After some basic safety and sanitary guidelines and a quick demonstration, we were given the go-ahead to get cooking.

On the menu for the evening was salad with a vinaigrette dressing, garlic knots, linguine with roasted garlic and peppers, and Tres Leches cake. It sounded fancy and above my skill level, but I trusted that beginner's level really meant beginner's level. Plus, having a chef instruct us step-by-step reassured me we'd have an edible meal by the end of class.

As we cooked, I observed the other students. "Sometimes I like to guess people's backstories. Do you ever do that?" I asked.

"Like why do you think that couple is here?" Eric asked as he handed me a knife, chopping board and the garlic. His head jerked to the right and his eyes looked in the direction of the couple at the next station.

"Um." I didn't know. I looked at the couple he was referring to. Older, round, and watching the chef intently. "Recent retirees, bored and need a new hobby. They've decided to take up cooking," I suggested.

Once the garlic was chopped, Eric heated olive oil in a pan to sauté it.

"I agree. They need something to do with all their free time. Maybe he doesn't like golfing and she doesn't like bridge," he said.

"Or maybe they do, but decided to work on a new hobby."

He leaned in close and angled his head to the right. I caught a hint of something on his skin, maybe the scent of cedar. Whatever it was, I liked it.

"How about the couple at the front table?"

I followed his sightline to a couple at the front table closest to the door. She was wearing skintight jeans, high-heels and a top that revealed her voluptuous cleavage. Her bleach blond hair was piled high on top of her head in a carefully coiffed "messy" bun. Her acrylic nails kept hitting against the stainless-steel work surface, clacking every time. The husband was in jeans and a t-shirt. He kept checking his phone, then his wife would elbow him and he'd slide it back into his front pocket.

"Wife is keeping up with the Joneses, husband is bored and doesn't care." I continued my assessment. "He's only here because she wants to be here, but I don't think she really wants to cook, she just wants him to pay attention to her. He looks like he'd rather be anywhere but here. Maybe even working."

"Where does he work?" Eric asked.

I made a show of trying to get a better idea by observing what I could see of him. "A job that leaves him deeply dissatisfied with life. Maybe it's mundane. Maybe he's a supervisor at a store. Or in banking."

"I think you're right. You're pretty good at this."

I winked at him. "Someday we might even make detective on the force."

"We've got mad skills," he said. "Do you think anyone else is guessing what we're doing here?"

"Possibly. Hopefully they can focus on cooking and chopping and not guessing why we're here. We're just good at multitasking," I quipped back.

"Right, 'cause our last cooking experience turned out so well." We busted out laughing, resulting in a stern look from Chef Michael. I felt like I was back in high school. It wasn't just the classroom setting and the teacher, but that giddy feeling of having a crush on a boy.

We continued on while we added peppers to the garlic, and finally sauce. That simmered while we focused on the fettucine.

I leaned in close and whispered, "What's our story, Mr. Future Police Detective?" I may also have inhaled his delicious scent.

"We're just two cool kids who don't know how to cook,

dating, trying to up our desirability skills," he said, his voice low.

"Because the way to a man's stomach is—" I started laughing again.

"That's right. The best way to my stomach is through my mouth."

Our laughter resulted in another stern look from Chef Michael. Gordon Ramsey he was not, thank goodness, but his displeasure was not lost on me. "That's exactly what I meant. No, really, a way to a man's heart is through his stomach," I said.

His cute, crooked smile appeared. "Or her stomach." He paused. "Did it work? Have I made it through to your heart?"

Time seemed to slow down as he looked over at me and our eyes met. My heart raced, the corners of my lips turned up and I leaned in close to his ear.

"It's working," I whispered.

27

Monday morning, I was back at the grind. I swiveled in the chair at the drafting table, staring daggers at Sweden, while I pretended to work. Deadlines were dangerously close, and yet here I was, distracted. I should've been focused on maps, but instead, I was thinking about men. I glanced at my phone—it was about time for a break, so I allowed myself to indulge in my thoughts.

I was dating two men. How did this happen? How did I *let* it happen? I'd never had this happen. Ever. I was lucky if I had one man in my life, and sometimes I didn't even have that.

When Abba starting singing from my phone, I thanked myself for assigning that ringtone to Maddox. At least now I had a heads up about which man was calling me.

"Hello?" I answered quickly.

"Elsie?" The smooth deep voice of Maddox greeted me.

My pulse quickened as soon as I heard his voice. I hated that that was my automatic response whenever I talked to him. What if I sounded as nervous as I felt? Why couldn't I seem as cool, calm and collected as he was? "Yes."

"How are you?"

"Stressed but okay," I said.

"Stressed? About what?" He sounded like my answer was a total surprise.

"Yeah, you know, maps and things," I said. "How's Cowboy the Cat?"

"We've officially shortened his name to Cowboy. He's had shots and has remained in hiding since he got here. I know he's alive because his food gets eaten."

"I assume he has to adjust to being rehomed, but hopefully he'll settle in soon," I said.

"Let's hope so," he said. "Are you free right now?"

Was I free? Conveniently, yes! I forced my voice to remain steady. "Sure."

"I realize it's last minute, but I had a cancellation in my schedule. Do you want to grab lunch?" His confidence oozed through the phone.

My stomach grumbled. When was the last time I ate? In fact, I was starving. I justified going out to eat, because if I didn't eat, I would die. "Yes! How soon?"

"I'm getting in my car right now."

That was a little *too* soon, but I could make it work.

It was a scramble to get ready, which seemed to be the norm with going out with him. I yanked off my sweats and kicked them across the room. I pulled on jeans and a sweater (checked to make sure it wasn't on inside out and backwards), applied deodorant, ran a brush through my hair and tamed it into a braid.

On my mad dash to the door, I did notice the small, fake Christmas tree set up in Nana's living room. When had that gone up? Had Nana put that up? Or Vivian? Or both of them? Somehow time was still moving forward despite my not participating in life outside of my room.

I made it to the front door just as he rang the doorbell.

"Hey," I said, a little out of breath. "I'm ready."

"You look beautiful," he said, once we were settled in the Tesla.

"Thanks," I said, then glanced in the visor mirror and realized, in horror, I hadn't put any makeup on. Had he noticed?

"We're not jaunting off in the helicopter to New York City, are we?"

He chuckled. "Not today. I have an hour and a half, so we'll have to be quick. How about lobster rolls?"

"Seafood always sounds good," I said. "I've missed seafood while I've been living in Vegas."

"But there were world-class restaurants on the Strip."

"I don't frequent the Strip or those restaurants too often. Too expensive and too much of a hassle to get there. And I don't trust 'fresh' grocery store seafood."

"New York City will have to be a date for another day," he said. "How long did you say you'd be here for?"

"I don't exactly know. I'll stay through Christmas, of course. Who doesn't like to be with their family for the holidays?"

He paused ever-so-slightly. "I know a few people."

"You?"

"No, not me. I have some stepfamily who aren't so, copacetic with holidays."

"Are they ... not copaseptic?"

He tried not to smile. "Copacetic."

"That's what I said."

"You said 'copaseptic'. Like septic, like the tank."

"So having stepfamily visit for the holidays can make the

day take a septic turn." I tried to dig myself out of my mistake without admitting it. I wasn't doing it very gracefully.

He put his hand on mine after he turned into the parking lot of the restaurant. "Clever, but I'm going to say nice try."

"Okay, you caught me," I said as we held hands and walked to the entrance. "You'll have to tell me about your family dynamics some time."

"I will. Promise. Next time. But you've been warned."

Alarm bells went off in my head. "Are they awful people? I mean, I find that hard to believe when you're such a nice guy."

"My dad's on his fourth wife."

"Oh."

"And there's lots of stepsiblings because of that. And stepmoms and half-siblings. Let's say our family tree is like the bramble of a bush. It's a mess."

"Every family can technically be a mess. Depends on the situation and when it happens."

We ordered at the counter, got our lobster rolls and slid into a booth, opposite each other. I liked looking at him. He took a bite of his sandwich. "This is really good."

I nodded. Lobster rolls were a must anytime I came to town.

He continued. "But let's not ruin our lunch with talk of my family. We were talking about how long you're in town for."

Like I had told him, it wasn't completely decided. "After the holidays, I'd love to move back to Las Vegas. But the thought of driving cross-country *again* is exhausting. The possibility of driving through snowstorms also terrifies me."

"Why don't you ship the car and fly?"

I took a bite of my lobster roll while I considered his suggestion. It would be the easiest solution, if only my bank account would stop laughing at me and telling me "no".

"Financially, I'm not in the position to do that right now. Maybe closer to spring, and I'll have to find an apartment and another roommate." I told him some more about my current situation with my roommate and the apartment. "Everything's a bit undecided."

"Sounds like it. So, you don't have any concrete plans, yet?" he asked.

"Nope."

His eyebrows went up. "Is there a chance I could persuade you to stay a past the holidays?"

What exactly did he mean by that? Was he looking for something more long term?

"I don't know," I said weakly. "I haven't thought that far ahead."

Did I want to be in a relationship? Since *Desperately Seeking Mrs. Right*, I'd sworn off men for a while. And also swore I would never date a man again who was dating more than one woman. But here I was, a woman, dating more than one man. My, how the tables had turned.

He wiped his mouth with the napkin and then held up his glass of water as if making a toast. "Well, then, for the record, I hope you're around after the holidays and that we get to see a lot more of each other."

It sounded like he was making plans. Was I supposed to clink my water glass with him to show I concurred?

The alarm on his phone went off, interrupting the moment. "And that is my signal that I've got to get back to work."

Someone walked by and accidentally bumped the table, causing Maddox to spill his coffee. "Crap!" he said, grabbing at the pile of napkins. "I just bought these." He blotted his pants, then sighed loudly. "I better go clean this up before it stains. Either way, it's going to look like I wet my pants. Will you still be okay being seen with me?"

"Of course. Now, if you really wet your pants, I might not answer that so quickly."

He threw me a smile and headed to the bathroom in the back corner of the restaurant.

The doorbell jangled and I happened to look over my shoulder, distracted by the noise. "Hi, Officer McCutty," the girl behind the counter called out as he walked in.

I froze, then sunk down in my seat. I contorted my body to get a better view through the latticework wall that divided the entrance from the dining. My heart raced. I felt like I'd been caught doing something wrong.

Maybe he wouldn't see me. Maybe he wouldn't be in here very long—just in and out to pick up a to-go order. Maybe he wouldn't—he looked over his shoulder and recognition passed on his face.

He approached the table. "Hey, Elsie. I thought that was you. How are you?" He loomed over me. There was a plate full of food across from me on the table. It didn't take a detective to figure out I was not alone.

I cleared my throat. "Taking a lunch break."

"Still working on Sweden?"

"Yes. I've almost eaten through the five-pound bag of Swedish fish you gave me. How about you? How are you?"

"So far, so good. We still on for tomorrow?"

I smiled despite myself. "Yes. Still good."

"Great. I'm looking forward to it."

Before I had a chance to add "me too," Maddox came up behind him.

"Excuse me," Maddox said. He pointed to the chair Eric blocked.

Eric sidestepped to clear a path for Maddox. "Oh, hey man, sorry."

Had Maddox overheard our conversation about tomorrow?

"Good to see you again," Maddox said. It sounded almost like a dismissal.

Eric's eyes swept the table, glancing between me and Maddox. A hurt look passed over his face, but was gone just as quick.

Please don't ask if I'm on a date. Please don't ask if I'm on a date. Eric had every right to ask if I was on a date. I'd tell him, but later.

"So, uh ..." There was an awkward pause as I tried to think of a way to complete the sentence and wrap up this situation.

Eric tapped his index finger on the table twice as if fidgeting while he was thinking. "I'll, uh, see you later, Elsie. Nice seeing you again." He waved, then headed for the door, his coffee tray in hand.

"You two still hang out?" Maddox asked, adjusting his seat at the table.

The wooden chair I was sitting on suddenly became super uncomfortable. I shifted my weight, trying to find a better position. "Yeah."

"More than friends?"

I twisted my lips. How to qualify it? "Yeah."

Maddox stilled for a moment. He then cleared his throat. "Meaning he's the competition." His watch lit up again, but he didn't even glance at it.

I snorted. I didn't think his observation was reality. "Um,

no, I wouldn't say that." Not yet, at least. Possibly? Who knew what the future would hold?

"You're dating me. You're dating him. Eventually you'll have to choose."

I forced my expression to remain neutral. "It's not exclusive or serious with him or you."

"Yet," Maddox interrupted.

"Yet," I agreed. "But right now, I consider myself casually dating. It's really too soon to make that decision."

"How will you know?"

Good question. I never thought I'd be dating two guys at once. But a handful of dates, with two separate guys, didn't necessarily constitute a relationship with either of them. I felt like it was still in the beginning stages, where you still wanted to work out if you wanted to keep dating.

"I don't know—"

He blinked.

"Three to five dates," I threw out, not really having thought it through.

"We've been on three. One more and you'll know?" he asked. I could tell by the way his eyebrow quirked that he was serious.

"It's not a hard and fast rule. I learned from my time with Joshua that fast's not always good and sooner isn't always better. I want to take my time—see if we're a good fit—before we make it official."

"We're a good fit."

"Why?" It was a genuine question that I wanted to know his answer.

"Because." He shrugged. "You check all the boxes on my checklist."

His answer surprised me. Did he have a short checklist? Or a really random one? Because, let's be honest here, the guy was a billionaire and I didn't consider myself anything special. "You have a checklist?"

"That sounds worse than it is. Don't you have a list of certain qualities you want to find in a person you're dating? It's not a bad thing. And for me, you're that person."

Whoa. This was happening way too fast for my liking.

His phone buzzed, but he quickly silenced it without taking his eyes off me.

It was easy to feel that way at the beginning of a relationship. That was when you were happiest, most agreeable and trying to be everything he wanted you to be. But like everything else I learned on *Desperately Seeking Mrs. Right*, you couldn't fake who you really were once you got past the initial honeymoon phase of dating.

Right now, Maddox and I were still in the honeymoon phase of dating.

We stood to leave. "Dates four and five will blow you away," he said.

Would that be a good thing or a bad thing?

28

I stared into the depths of Nana's fridge. It didn't have anything good. I was all out of Swedish fish and steam. Why was I looking for something to munch on? I was going out with Eric and we'd probably get food. But I wanted chocolate. Or chips. Or something to use up some of my nervous energy.

"Nana, do you have any chocolate bars?"

"If I do, it's probably so old it's grown hair on it," Nana called back.

She was in the living room, in her recliner, a fleece blanket over her lap watching *Golden Girls*. "See, this is one of the perks of living in your own home. You can watch what you want, when you want, with the volume as high as you want."

I sat on the couch and turned my attention to the window.

The TV paused. "Whatcha thinking about, dear?" Nana asked.

I'd been anticipating my date with Eric since yesterday. Sweden had suffered, but I had soldiered on, working through the rest of the day. I assumed there'd be a conversation about the incident in the café with Maddox. Whether it was right away, a little later in the date, or maybe even a later date, I'd have to face it and was not looking forward to it. If it was me, I'd definitely want to know what the deal was. And sooner than later.

"I had lunch with Maddox yesterday and ran into Eric, who I have a date with tonight. Actually, he's picking me up in the next few minutes."

"How'd he seem?"

"Like he knew I was on a date." Would he be upset? Probably. I would be, which made me feel more pressured to make a decision and soon.

"What are you going to do about it?" Nana asked.

"Choose."

~

WHEN ERIC DID PULL up to Nana's house, he was in the squad car. And still in his uniform. *Weird.* Was he running late?

I opened the door as he was about to knock on the door. "Hey," I said.

He thumbed over his shoulder toward the car. "I have to cancel. I got called into work."

"Do you have a minute to come in?"

I could tell by his stone-like expression he wasn't interested in coming in.

"I really have to get going," he said.

"Okay. Let's reschedule."

He shifted his stance. "You're dating Maddox Wellington?"

I exhaled the breath I'd been holding. The air was so

cold it came out as a white, billowing puff. There it was. I'd worried for good reason.

"Yes."

"You're dating both of us?"

That was worth a lip-twisting pause. "Yes. I told you I was dating other people."

"But of all the people you could date, why him?"

Did he know something I didn't? "Is there something wrong with him?"

"I don't trust him. He's a shark when it comes to the business world, why not dating?"

I hadn't seen that side of Maddox, not even a little. "What do you mean?"

Eric threw his hands in the air. "He thinks he can come to town and start building it up. Maybe we don't want his 'vision of growth' for our town." He made air quotes.

"Oh my gosh! Why are we having this conversation outside? It's freezing! Seriously, come in."

"I don't want to come in."

Okay, looked like we were doing it outside. "And for the record, he doesn't seem shady," I said.

He shook his head slowly. "I just don't like him. He always has a smirk on his face like he's going to win."

I didn't know he and Maddox had that much interaction. Was there stuff I didn't know about? "It's not a competition!"

Eric squinted at me. "It's not?"

What was it with men and competition? Everything in life was not a competition. "I'm not doing it to pit you against each other or to try and create a 'bidding war'."

"Guys like him, it's always a competition. Girls, business, life. They want to win, whatever it is, whatever the cost."

"That's not the vibe I get from him. At least not on the dates I've gone on with him."

Yes, he seemed to go to extremes when it came to our date, the flowers and Cowboy, but none of it seemed to be in a negative way.

"Is it serious?"

"I haven't gone on enough dates with either of you to feel like it's serious."

"Good to know."

"I went into this just wanting to have fun. I told you that from the beginning. I didn't plan on getting serious with anyone." *Or two.* Call me crazy! "When I dated Joshua, there were so many girls competing for his affection. It's not fun to be in a situation like that, nor is it fair. I'm not trying to do that. I'm trying to get to know each of you." The dating show wanted to created drama. I wanted to discourage it. Did I really think I could keep dating two guys in two separate worlds in one very small town? "I'm not into games. I've been involved in that on the show, and I'm not going to do that. I realize being in a relationship with someone means I'm involved in their life and I'm not about to mess with someone's life. I'm being as honest and sincere as I can be."

He leaned forward with an expectant look on his face. "You realize you're going to have to choose, right?"

Of course, I realized it. But who? It was the million, or billion, dollar question. I liked them both, and were both great guys for different reasons. Ugh. I hated admitting that someday, soon, I'd have to choose between them. Which also meant I'd have to break up with one of them. Or maybe even both, and go from 2-0 just like that. Or they could break up with me. I never imagined I'd be in a situation like this.

"I do."

"Let me know what you decide," he said, then returned to the squad car.

I shut the door a little harder than necessary. I watched through the window as Eric drove away before giving in to my frustration.

"Aaaaaaaagh!"

Nana appeared in the hallway. "Are you calling me, honey?"

"No. I'm letting out a primal scream of frustration," I said.

"Will you teach me how to do it?"

That was unexpected. "What?"

"You know, the primal scream of frustration. It sounds like a good method to release some tension."

Maybe Nana was onto something. "I don't think there's a specific way to do it. I just screamed out my frustration."

"What are you frustrated about?"

"Men," I said automatically.

"What?"

"Men," I repeated.

"Let me hear you scream it," she said louder.

"MEN!" I yelled.

"Louder," she called.

"MEN!" I screamed. "WHY ARE THEY SO COMPLICATED?"

"BEING BABYSAT!" Nana yelled.

I turned and looked at her. "What?"

She blinked at me, perfectly calm. "That's what I'm frustrated about. Everyone constantly thinks I need to be babysat."

I walked to her and took her hand. "We want you to be safe."

"I know, but I'm much happier here, living with you."

"Thanks, Nana."

"Now let's go get some ice cream and figure out this man problem. If one bowl doesn't do it, then two should."

I wasn't going to argue about the ice cream, but I wasn't going to let Nana have two bowls, either. I couldn't deal with my love life and her life slipping into a diabetic coma at the same time.

29

We had just pulled out the ice cream and the bowls, when the front door shut. Vivian appeared in the kitchen seconds later. She eyed the carton of chocolate cookie crumble and the bowls on the counter. "Ooh, ice cream. Even though it's freezing outside, I still want some." She peeled off her winter coat and hung it over the back of a chair. "What's the occasion?"

"A love life powwow," Nana said, completely serious.

Once we dished our ice cream, we sat down around the kitchen table.

"Now, tells us exactly what the problem is Elsie, so we know what we're dealing with," Nana stated, as if formally calling a meeting to order.

"I'm dating two men," I started. "Both of them are such nice guys."

"Such nice guys? Such nice guys? That's all you have to say about them?" Vivian sounded shocked.

"Well, it's true," I said.

"And you don't want that nice guy to finish last, dear, do you?" Nana asked.

It wasn't even a problem of the nice guy finishing last. It wasn't that one was an underdog, at least in my eyes. "No. I'm just having a hard time choosing between them. They are both literally nice guys that have great qualities"

"You're well beyond that. You should be seeing fireworks at this point," Vivian said.

Nana sprinkled her hands in the air, pantomiming fireworks.

What kind of guys was Vivian dating? Fireworks? Maybe on *Desperately Seeking Mrs. Right,* you'd get literal fireworks after a date, but everything on that show was so over-the-top and unrealistic.

"We've been on three dates or so. That's too soon to fall for someone." Another thing I'd learned on the dating show.

She took a bite. "What makes Maddox a 'nice guy'?" She pointed at me with her spoon. "I want specifics."

I held my palms up. "He just is. I don't know. I like him. I enjoy spending time with him. But I don't know him enough to be in love."

"He's perfect. How can you not see that? He's rich, he's attractive, and he's an animal lover. I'd be in love with him."

I was firm. "Nope. Too soon. I've learned my lesson about rushing into a relationship."

"But what if you're passing up a good thing? Or maybe the perfect thing? You'll regret it."

Those were not questions I was ready to entertain yet. "If I take my time, then I'll get to know him and will realize if I'm passing up a good thing or not."

"You're eventually going to have to choose between the guys," Vivian said. Her words sounded hauntingly familiar.

I sighed. "I know. I just don't know who."

"Let me go get my Betty Whiteboard," Nana said. "Writing it down always helps me."

Nana disappeared into one of the bedrooms and came back almost immediately carrying a board and a dry erase marker. She placed it in the middle of the table and handed Vivian the marker. "You be the scribe."

"Okay," Vivian said. "Call things out."

She wrote as I spoke, the marker squeaking on the surface. In the end, we'd compiled what I considered to be a thorough list.

<u>Eric's Pros</u>
Looks good in a uniform
Handsome
Nice guy
We both suck at cooking
We have fun together
Great kisser
I feel relaxed around him
Has a house
<u>Eric's Cons</u>
He's a cop. He could get shot
He won't make as much money as Maddox
Might want to stay in small town forever
He's a bad cook
<u>Maddox's Pros</u>
Billionaire
Good-looking
Nice guy
Animal lover
Has house help/hires people to do things
Has money, will travel
<u>Maddox's Cons</u>
Workaholic

Everything is always a rush
Everything has to be over-the-top
Feel stressed when with him

On paper, it looked like Maddox's pros outweighed his cons and that his list outweighed Eric's. Putting down the good and the bad didn't make me feel better about either of them. It didn't help me decide on one over the other.

Vivian tapped the board with the marker cap on Maddox's name. "Personally, I wouldn't let him slip through my fingers," Vivian said.

"You think I'm letting him slip through my fingers?"

She nodded emphatically. "Yes. I'd be all over him. Lit-er-ally."

"Okay, don't get graphic. I get your point. But why?"

"Well, he's a billionaire."

"That's a lot of zeros," Nana added. "And he *is* a hottie." She winked and threw me an exaggerated smile. "But you know how the saying goes: Money does not equal happiness. Or is it money can't buy you love? Either way, money comes and goes. It shouldn't be the final deciding factor."

Money was attractive. And Maddox was attractive. "Besides the money, though," I said.

My sister's eyes opened wide. "Is there anything else?"

Nana broke in. "It comes down to how they treat you and how they make you feel. Like money, looks don't always last, either."

I pictured him in a smart tuxedo, like 007. It was a nice imaginary snapshot. "You're right. Looks can fade away, which is why I need to love him."

Vivian sighed dramatically.

"Eric's still in the running. He's a great guy too with a lot of great qualities." My heart pitter-patted as I spoke the words.

"He's not rich."

"No." That seemed to be the one sticking point with my sister.

"But Maddox," Vivian said, her voice dreamy. "Think of the potential. Travel, money, vacations, houses, money."

There was a lot of potential. "If I don't love him, all the money in the world wouldn't matter. I wouldn't want to spend the rest of my life with him."

"Living on a cop salary might be hard," Vivian said.

"I would work and contribute to our income. I'm a starving artist now, but we could make it work," I said.

"With Maddox, you wouldn't have to work."

"I don't know if I don't want to work."

"Really?" Vivian asked.

I could tell by her expression that she couldn't understand. In her mind, not working might seem ideal.

"What would I do if I didn't work?" Generally, I liked working. I liked my profession and the ability to create and be involved in art. I wasn't ready to give that up and even if I did, what would I do with myself? Doing nothing sounded boring.

"Shop."

"I don't see myself living a 'Kardashian' lifestyle. I need more to life than spending money."

A smile spread across her face. "You'd have Maddox."

"What if that's not enough?" What if Maddox didn't have enough time for me? He seemed like he was always working, even when he wasn't.

She held her hands as if she gave up. "Alright. I hope you know what you're doing."

Me too. But not rushing wasn't a bad thing. As long as it didn't lead to dragging my feet, which *was* a bad thing—there was a fine line between them.

I just wasn't quite ready to make the decision between the two guys. I told myself one more date with each of them and then I'd decide. Just to be sure.

Nana came over to me and wrapped her arms around me. "Don't doubt yourself too much. You'll make the right decision."

I put my arms over hers. "Thanks, Nana."

30

"Wahoo!" I screamed to no one in particular as I sat back in the office chair. This was the best Thursday ever! I had just finished the map of Sweden and it gave me much cause to celebrate. "Two down, one to go! Paris, here I come!"

I stood up, did a little happy dance, shook the stiffness from my joints and left my ~~prison~~ bedroom to take a break. I grabbed my phone on the way out and headed for the kitchen. I was hungry!

Nana sat in her recliner, happy as a clam, with remote in hand and *The Golden Girls* reruns on the TV. Seeing her content made me happy.

Nana looked up over the back of the chair. "Did you finish, dear?"

I nodded my stiff neck. "Finally."

"What are you going to do next? Take a nap?"

I wish. "I have to package this up and get it to FedEx ASAP."

"Then will you take a nap?"

"Maybe a catnap." Saying that made me think of

Cowboy. I wondered if Maddox had sent any new pictures of him. I turned my phone on as I grabbed a bottle of water and carton of yogurt. With all the junk food I'd been eating lately, something on the healthier side would do me some good.

The dings kept coming as my phone blew up with texts.

Maddox had sent a photo dump-worth of pictures, all of the cat. I found it both sweet and humorous how much he had taken to owning Cowboy. It warmed my heart to know Cowboy would live the rest of his life being cared for.

Maddox: Wanna go Christmas shopping?

Maddox: Do you have time to get something to eat?

Maddox sent a pic of Cowboy, playing with some yarn.

Me: Cowboy looks so happy! Still working hard, can't go shopping and don't have time to grab food. I'll text you when I have some time.

My ex-roommate also had texted, updating me on the boyfriend situation.

Jade: Rob doesn't want me leaving my shaving cream can in the shower. He says it leaves rust rings on the basin. Doesn't he ever give it a break? It literally says on the can, 'Rust-free container'.

Me: Where does he leave his shaving cream? Under the sink?

Jade: He has an electric shaver.

Me: Oh. He's pretty particular about certain things it seems like.

Jade: Seems like everything. I was so happy I had to leave for work this morning before he could finish his lecture on rust rings.

Me: Yuck

Jade: Maybe being a neat freak isn't as nice as I thought it'd be. I thought I wouldn't have to clean. Turns out I'm living with a hairy version of Mr. Clean.

I laughed out loud at the picture I conjured in my head. Mr. Clean with Bob Ross hair. Even though I had met her boyfriend and knew that wasn't an accurate image, it was still funny.

Me: Does he wear tight, white pants when he cleans?

Jade: Ha ha! No. I don't think he owns white pants, but if he did, they'd be spotless.

Me: Ironed with a crease down the front of the leg.

Jade: Yup! Navy Style.

Me: Sounds like you need to make a decision. It doesn't seem like you want to be in a long-term relationship with him.

Jade: Is it that obvious?

Me: Yeah, it kind of is.

Jade: Found a roommate or apartment yet?

Me: Not yet. Still looking.

Jade: Maybe we should move back in together.

The irony was we were both in the situations we were in because she wanted to move out. She wasn't a bad person, just looking for love like the rest of us.

I wasn't sure I was desperate enough to take her up on her offer yet, but that decision was packed away with the rest of the things I couldn't deal with right now.

One thing I needed to deal with, but didn't know how, was Eric.

I hadn't texted him and he hadn't texted me.

A little ball of disappointment grew in my stomach if I thought about it too long. But I couldn't worry about that now. Sweden had to be sent off and Paris started before my deadlines crushed me.

I wrapped my scarf around me and left for FedEx.

31

I gripped my steering wheel while anticipation squeezed my stomach. I had the heat blasting so high, I could feel sweat forming under my scarf. My nerves also contributed to the perspiration. I was on my way to see Maddox, and it felt almost like a first date. I was entering unknown territory, otherwise known as his house.

It was really my own fault. I had initiated this by texting him and offering to drop the remaining cat treats off at his place for Cowboy ~~the Cat~~. That, in turn, was answered with a "yes" and a time frame that would work for him.

GPS guided me to the other side of town, onto streets I'd never driven, let alone knew existed. I was almost to the end of a dead-end street, when a driveway appeared on the right side of the street, just beyond a pine tree. I exhaled; I was not being misled by my phone.

I turned in, only to be greeted by a gate. I buzzed the buzzer and a few seconds later, the gates creaked open, allowing me entrance.

A massive, modern house with a circular driveway came into view, surrounded by trees and a manicured yard.

I felt a resurge of anxiety as I approached the set of oversized front doors. They were two panels of wrought iron and frosted glass and did nothing to make me feel welcome. I half expected the doorbell to sound like something that would belong to Dracula's castle. Luckily, it was a plain and simple, loud, melodious *ding dong ding ding*.

Maddox's housekeeper (I assumed?), an older, gray-haired woman, appeared behind the massive, oversized door. Somehow, I had expected Alfred from *Batman* to answer the door.

She opened the door wide enough to let me pass, probably because it was so cold outside, and shut the door quickly behind me. "Mr. Wellington is in his office. You can go in, he's expecting you."

Having never been in Maddox's house, I stood there, frozen in place, clutching my bag of cat goodies. "I don't know where that is."

She led me down the wide hallway to the first door on the right.

Even with him expecting me, I still felt the need to knock lightly on the door before I let myself in.

I took in the large room, which was completely different than my bedroom/office space. His was wide open, with bookshelves lining the wall, a huge glass and metal desk, with maybe five things on it. I thought of my desk, covered in paper, eraser crumbs, pencil shavings and empty cups. My plan was to clean up before I finished.

He wasn't at his desk, but on a sleek, black leather sofa, with his computer on his lap.

"Hey," I said.

He glanced up and quickly snapped shut his laptop.

"Whatcha doing over there?" I asked, mainly curious

because of his knee-jerk reaction. The array of sites he could be perusing that he wouldn't want me to see ran through my mind: his bank accounts, investment funds, dating sites (let's hope not), Facebook (was he ashamed?), Instagram, his company's website, or an inappropriate website (let's *definitely* hope not).

"Nothing," he automatically responded. Not only did he act like I'd caught him doing something he shouldn't be doing, but he sounded like I had caught him doing something he shouldn't be doing.

"Nothing?" I teased. "You don't act like it's nothing." Now I really wanted to know. I even started devising a plan in my mind how I could get a glimpse of what was on his computer. Wait until he fell asleep? Feed him turkey so he got sleepy? Peek when he used the bathroom? Really, it was none of my business, but it felt like he was keeping secrets from me.

"Just some, uh, working on a side—" he paused, "it's work-related stuff. Nothing important." He shrugged to confirm it.

He treated everything to do with work as a priority. There was no way what he was doing was unimportant if it was work-related.

"Uh-huh," I said, slowly, suspiciously. I totally did not believe him.

He stood up quickly, walked over to me and enveloped me in a hug. "But enough about that, we don't need to let work interfere with our visit."

Weird, because it always seemed to interfere with our dates.

I followed him out of his office, noticing he provided a steady stream of chatter about mostly nothing.

What was he so nervous about?

There was something Maddox clearly didn't want me knowing about.

"Did you see the cat when you came in?" He motioned me to follow him further down the hall.

"No. I came straight to your office," I said.

His phone ringing interrupted our conversation.

"Hold on, I've got a call, and then I want to ask you something," he said quickly and lifted his phone.

I waited for about thirty seconds while he took the call, checking out his house from where I stood. It was cavernous, but not in a dark way, with high ceilings, marble tile floors and pillars marking the separation of areas in the open floor plan.

"Sorry about that," Maddox said, returning his attention to me as he slipped his phone into his pocket. "Come say hello to Cowboy."

I held up the bag of treats I'd brought. "I'd love to see Cowboy," I said, forcing myself to use his edited name. "These are for him."

Maddox veered to the right and we entered a large room with high ceilings and a huge window overlooking the front yard and driveway.

"You've got to see what I got for him," Maddox said, full of enthusiasm.

The room was filled with all of the things we had bought on the shopping trip: cat toys, a scratching post, an activity center and a hammock. There was also a cat condo that must have been purchased since the shopping trip. It was mostly void of furniture—human furniture—that is, except for a black, leather recliner chair. Beside it was a miniature version of an arm chair with black and white fabric. The colors reminded me of Cowboy's hair. Beside the smaller chair, was Cowboy, stretched out, napping in the sun shining in from the window.

I pointed to the mini chair. "Fancy little chair you've got there," I said. I wanted to know the story behind the miniature chair that the cat wasn't sitting in.

He rubbed his chin. "Yeah. I buy him the top-of-the line kid's chair and he won't sleep on it, just next to it."

"Maybe he's making sure it's not a real cow before he claims it as his own?" I didn't know enough about cats to offer any real advice. But picturing Cowboy in his little cow chair was totally cute.

"He always sits in my chair, to the point that I try to sit and he won't move. Since I don't want to sit on him, I thought the best solution was to get him his own chair. And now he only sits near it, not *in* it."

"Is it a scent thing? Do you need to rub yourself all over it so it has your scent?" I asked.

"Can you picture me rubbing myself on the chair? Really?"

Actually, I could.

He continued. "Or even trying to sit in it? My massive frame would crush the chair to splinters." A smile followed.

I laughed. "Don't go breaking his chair."

"I won't go breaking his chair," he sang sing-songy, reminiscent of the song in *Grease*.

I took a closer look at the chair. "What about a dirty T-shirt? Well, not dirty, but worn and not washed. You know, so it has your scent on it."

"I don't want his chair to smell like B.O."

Maddox did *not* smell like B.O., at least not when I was around him. "It wouldn't. It'd just smell like you. I like the way you smell."

"Oh, yeah?" his voice was low. Sexy.

I felt the surge of anticipation. Excitement gripped my stomach as he closed the distance between us and his lips found mine. Finally, a real kiss.

This is...weird, I thought, as our lips touched. His lips felt wet and...sloppy. *Wait. This isn't how a first kiss is supposed to go.* I'd been anticipating it being different. *Way* different. *This has to get better. It's awkward. Like most first kisses. It'll get more passionate*, I reassured myself. I reached up, tangling my hand in his hair, hoping that'd get me more in the moment.

It didn't.

I abruptly pulled away.

"Hey, what's going on?" he said, his hand brushing my hair away from my face.

I shook my head, taking in a deep breath. "Nothing. Just, wow, that was, uh, some kiss." I hoped my response covered up for my strange behavior.

A smile spread across his face. "It was."

His phone rang, interrupting the moment. "Sorry. Again," he said as he looked at the screen.

"I know, I know. You've got to take it," I said as he walked out of the room to have the conversation in private.

"It's just you and me, Cowboy," I said to the sleeping cat. I sighed and sat beside him on the floor in front of the human-sized leather recliner. I reached over and gave him a gentle pet between the ears. I didn't know how receptive he'd be to being woken up, so I proceeded with caution.

Cowboy's eyes opened slowly and he stretched, spreading his paws.

Footsteps from down the hall signaled Maddox's return. "Sorry about that," he said, and stood directly in front of me. "Now, where were we?"

The moment had passed and it wasn't like we could pick up where we had left off, making out like two high school kids.

I stood and brushed myself off. "Well, we were talking—"

A smile slowly appeared, seductively. "I'm not talking about the talking—"

Did I go with the flirting and try to rekindle the "moment", or just—

"Meow," Cowboy said, getting up also.

It was the out I needed.

"Cowboy seems to be doing really well," I said, turning my attention, and hopefully the conversation, to him.

Maddox looked at the cat, and then at me. "He's great. I couldn't ask for a better cat. He's affectionate, but not clingy. Independent and not needy."

"Everything you'd want in a girlfriend." I offered a wide, cheesy smile.

He shook his head. "No. I have much higher expectations for my girlfriends. While my cat's qualities would make for great girlfriend qualities, I'd need more out of my relationship with my girlfriend."

I spread my arms wide and rotated, as if taking in his whole room. "You're not going to settle in life and become a crazy cat man, surrounding yourself with felines for companionship?"

"I sure hope not. I aspire for more."

I wondered if I would be enough for him and his aspirations.

"Which leads me to my next question."

My heart raced and I broke out into a little sweat. *Oh no! Was he going to ask me to be his girlfriend?* Here I thought I'd be the one making the decision between the two men, but he was taking charge. Panic fluttered in my throat. I wasn't ready to just decide right here and now.

"Want a drink first?"

32

He motioned toward the living room. It was large, open and had a wall of windows overlooking the waterfront. Cowboy followed us in. As soon as we were seated, he jumped up on my lap and demanded head scratches by rubbing his head into my shoulder.

"Um, sure, water?" I said, distracted by Cowboy and the view. "This is gorgeous. I could look at that for hours."

"Then stay as long as you want and admire the view with me."

He handed me a chilled Perrier and an empty glass. "Have a seat."

His sofa was a buttery-soft, brushed fabric of sorts, with cushions that had to be down-filled. "Thank you," I said, lifting the water to pour myself a glass.

As if on cue, his phone rang and he did the familiar finger signal of "one second" to signify he had to take that call. As he left the room, I turned my attention to Cowboy, trying to distract me from my thoughts. He had something he wanted to ask me, but hadn't. What was it? I was covered in cat hair from all the petting by the time Maddox returned.

He sat down beside me and put his hand on my knee. "I'd like you to be my date for my company's Christmas party," he said. His phone lit up at that exact moment. "Give it a rest," he muttered, sent the call to voicemail, and set his phone on the glass coffee table.

Relieved, I exhaled, my chest decompressing. "Sure." A company Christmas party was a pretty easy ask. That was easier to commit to than being his girlfriend.

"Great. Everyone is dying to meet you."

What had I just done?

I self-soothed by rubbing the smooth cloth of his couch.

Would his family be there? Who exactly was *dying* to meet me? "You mean co-workers?"

"Yeah. My friends. My business partners."

That was less stressful than meeting his family, but still stressful meeting his circle of people.

His phone rang again. This time he cursed and silenced it. It immediately rang again. I could see on the screen the name Sharene.

Sharene? "Who's Sharene?" I asked before I could stop myself.

"She's—" he shook his head and licked his lips, —"no one."

I gave him a sideways glance. "But she keeps calling. I feel like there's some big secret." My words came out in a huff. I stared past his feet at the marble floor.

"Secret?" he sounded genuinely surprised.

I shrugged, my shoulders sagging as I looked at him. "Like the way you acted slamming your computer shut and then all those phone calls. You obviously have something you don't want me to know about." I threw my hands up in the air.

He coughed a few times, clearing his throat. "I'm not keeping secrets. I'm just working on something that I'm not real confident about."

That was it? Hard to believe. "I can't imagine you not being confident about something."

He bowed his head. "Believe it or not, I'm not confident in every aspect of my life."

"I don't believe it." He oozed confidence. But then again, his performance trying to catch Cowboy didn't exactly scream confidence.

"Well, believe it." He paused, his mouth slightly open, as if he was unsure what to say next. "My friend asked me to officiate at his wedding."

I didn't mean to, but I started laughing as the image of Maddox wearing a priest's collar popped into my head. "Are you a minister? Is this something you did before you started your start-up? Officiated weddings?" I could kind of believe it.

"Nope, never officiated a wedding in my life. That's just it. I don't know why he asked me. I take relationships very seriously and I take this responsibility very seriously. It puts a lot of pressure on a guy."

"Does it? Why? Don't you just get up and read something and then pronounce them man and wife?"

"That's just it, they want me to write the ceremony. Like all the words. I want to make sure I say something important and profound and meaningful and it puts a lot of pressure on a guy like me that has never been married or been great with relationship advice. Ever."

"Oh, I see your dilemma." I tried not to laugh again, but couldn't help it.

"And I'm a bit of a perfectionist."

I nudged him with my elbow. "A bit?"

"Okay. I am."

"That and being a workaholic is how you got where you are today," I said. "It's only natural to want to give the best speech."

"Honestly, I don't really want to do it. But he's my best friend and this means a lot to him, so I agreed to do it."

Which was sweet. Doing something outside of his comfort zone because the person asking was important to him.

"But then his fiancée, Sharene," he lifted his chin toward his phone, "is basically a nightmare. Ever since they got engaged, she has turned into a bridezilla. She keeps calling me to *remind me*—" he made air quotes "—to get ordained and make sure all the paperwork is submitted well in advance."

"When do they get married?" I asked.

"That's just it. They haven't even set a date. All I know is she wants a destination wedding in the Bahamas. So that's the big secret. I've been asked to officiate a wedding and I know nothing about officiating."

I put my arm on his. "I'm sorry I jumped to conclusions."

"It's okay. She tends to go on nagging jags and today seems to be one of them."

"If it makes you feel any better, I don't know anything about officiating weddings, either."

He brightened. "Which actually leads me to one more question I have for you."

Uh-oh. Here goes. Here's the ask.

"Would you help me choose some art?"

I choked a little on a piece of ice. "Art?"

His eyes met mine and his mouth contorted into a cringy

expression. "Art, yeah. Because that's something you know about, but isn't really my thing. My financial planner keeps telling me I should invest in some art, but I find myself resisting. I don't want to pay a fortune to buy a canvas that has squiggly lines on it."

I thought up the wildest possibility I could. "What if those lines were made with ink derived from an octopus found in the deepest depths of the Marianna Trench? And that's why it was so valuable."

He pursed his lips and shook his head. "Still wouldn't make me want to pay that much money for it. And certainly not hang it on my wall. My decorator keeps telling me I need to decide what to hang on the walls and I really don't care."

"Oh." I couldn't imagine being able to afford a decorator at this point in my life.

"Maybe I should hire you to buy some art for me. Or advise me on some art investments."

I chewed on my lip while I thought of my response. "I don't know if I want that kind of responsibility. What if you hate everything I chose and you already paid for it? It's usually not returnable."

"That could happen," he said.

"Sounds like you need to find some art, or photography, that speaks to you. Maybe you need to look at more art or different mediums of art," I said.

He shrugged. "I don't really find art museums that exciting. I know I should, but I don't. I want to find it interesting because you find it interesting, but unless it's a piece in the Louvre, I generally don't find it all that interesting."

"Oh! The Louvre! I'm drawing a map of Paris right now. It's someplace I've always wanted to go. I was supposed to visit my senior year of college, but then I got mono and went home instead of France. Worst mistake of my life, kissing Richie Abelen."

"Is he the guy who gave you mono?"

"He was the only guy I kissed that semester. He gave it to me before we knew he was sick. He was better in no time, and I was sick for two months. Guess who got to go to Paris? Him. Not me." I added a pout for good measure.

"The Louvre is incredible. The building, the architecture. It's breathtaking." He looked off into the distance for a moment, as if enjoying a memory.

I had a small twinge of jealousy. But, on the plus side, we finally had something we could talk about easily. "That's one of my top ten travel bucket list items."

"What are your other places?" he asked.

"Other places in Paris, you know, all the touristy spots. I also want to go to Greece. It looks beautiful there. And Australia, but I'm not even sure why."

"Meaning?"

"I don't know. It seems like a cool place. Aside from the Opera House, I'm not sure what else I'd want to see there. But I love listening to Australians speak. I could close my eyes and listen to their accent forever."

"I haven't been. But it sounds like you want a cruise ship experience, where you can take day trips to see the sights."

"Maybe. I haven't been on a cruise. The only traveling I've done was with the reality show."

He took my hand and laced his fingers in with mine. "Where did you go on the show?"

"Grand Canyon, Disneyworld, Hawaii, and Belize." The last one was the final destination where the proposal was supposed to happen.

"But Paris is number one on your bucket list?"

"Yes. What's yours?"

"I don't really have a travel bucket list. I've done a lot of traveling. But Bali is one of my favorite places. Love it there. Love the laid-back culture. But we're not talking about my top ten, we're talking about yours. Where's the next place you think you'll go?"

"I don't know. But I have my passport ready at all times and will travel given the opportunity." Then I rolled my eyes. "It's wishful thinking because my financial bucket list is very different. It includes very boring, but adult, things such as pay off my student loans and start saving for a house."

He laughed, showing his perfect teeth. "The joys of adulting."

"Speaking of Paris, I've got to get going. The maps are calling me. I just finished Sweden and need to get working on Paris."

His phone chimed at the same time, and he shut off an alarm. "And I have a work call." With a quick kiss on the lips, he walked me to my car and said goodbye.

33

I went back into the cave for the next three and a half days, and focused on all things Paris. Every time I reached for a snack, I thought about Eric. How was he doing? If we were talking, what would he be dropping by to cheer me on? French fries? French toast? French pastries? Did he miss me as much as I missed him?

I pushed down the feelings, peeled a string cheese, and returned to my misery. Once the final map was done, I'd deal with the rest of my life—specifically finally making the choice between two great guys. Unless, of course, Eric's radio silence was his decision.

I swore never, ever to do this to myself again. Not with maps on a deadline or men in relationship.

When I emerged, with a completed map of Paris, I made the traditional trip to FedEx, where the employee greeted me by name and even gave me a candy cane. I came home, mass-ordered all my Christmas gifts on Amazon. Everyone —meaning Dad, Mom, Nana, Vivian, and my brother's family—was basically easy to shop for, especially with all the variety available. Maddox was another story. What do you buy for a man who can buy everything he wants already? And then there was Eric. What do you buy for a man who you care deeply about but might no longer care about you?

On a whim and a prayer, I bought something for Eric. It was non-returnable and a bit expensive for my budget, but I had just finished three maps in three weeks and my paycheck would be pretty big. I went ahead and splurged.

I spent a little more time searching the internet for gift ideas before getting too tired to keep my eyes open. I went to bed and slept twelve hours straight.

∽

As I slowly came out of my sleep coma, I became aware that the *beep* I kept hearing was actually my text notifications. I flung the comforter off my head and felt around for my phone on the nightstand next to me.

It was Jade, sending her set of daily complaints about her boyfriend.

I read through them but didn't start answering them right away. I scrolled through all of my notifications and messages.

Maddox had sent his daily photo dump of the cat.

I was too tired to respond or maybe just emotionally didn't feel like dealing with it. I really needed to deal with the Eric situation.

In a moment of bravado, or maybe I stupidity, I sent a text to Eric.

Me: How are you? I miss you.

When I didn't receive a message immediately, I was a little deflated. But maybe he was working. Maybe he would text later. Then I looked at the phone and realized it was after one in the morning. No wonder why he didn't respond —he was probably sleeping.

When my phone did light up and *ding*, I grabbed for it, hoping it was Eric. It wasn't. It was Jade.

Jade: New year's resolution. Do not move in with boyfriends.

Me: Things going bad?

Jade: The worst. I hate him. He's mean.

Me: Have you been drinking?

Jade: A little. Not a lot.

It sounded by her text that it might be more than a little, but not quite too much.

Me: Don't drive!

Jade: We're at his friend's party. Lives 5 mins away.

Me: Still. Don't drive.

Jade: OK. And I'm swearing at men.

Me: Swearing at or swearing off?

With the state she was in right now, it really could be either.

Jade: Done. No more boyfriend.

Me: Maybe wait until tomorrow to have that conversation.

Jade: Ok.

Me: Text me or call me later

Jade: Love ya!

I wondered, if things went south with Maddox or Eric or both of them, if I'd also be swearing off men for a while.

34

Maddox's company Christmas party was being held at the Encore Hotel overlooking Boston Harbor. Riding the elevator up, my anxiety ramped up a little with every passing floor.

Give it a chance, I told myself. *It might not be as bad as you're worrying about.*

I had a flashback to opening night on *Desperately Seeking Mrs. Right*. All the women, dressed in their best, hair done, jewelry flashing, exuding confidence and ready for fierce competition.

I was suddenly aware of how my shoe strap rubbed against the back of my heel and would probably end up being a blister by the end of the night. How my dress was a little too tight at the waistline and if I didn't hold my breath, I would bust a seam. That the spaghetti strap on the right shoulder kept falling off and the wires of my strapless bra dug into my rib cage. Would I be able to sit? Would I even be able to eat anything in this dress? Would I rip a seam or pass out from taking shallow breaths? This dress was gorgeous, but terribly uncomfortable.

The acrylic nails that I had done earlier in the afternoon made it impossible to do anything with my fingers that required attention to detail. The lash extensions weighed on my eyelids, an unexpected issue I hadn't anticipated. I was not used to this level of fancy for myself, even though it wasn't anything over the top. It looked good. Amazing, in fact, but strange to get used to. My updo pulled so tight at my hairline, it felt like my brain was being stretched and I could feel the start of a headache at my temples.

As the elevator opened, the elegant ballroom glittered before me and my stomach dropped. This was not a simple Christmas party with hors d'oeuvres and raffle prizes like I had tried to trick myself into believing. This was a party dripping in money, elegance and clout.

The restaurant was decorated like a winter wonderland. Everything was so sparkly, silver and shiny: from the huge chandeliers, to the ice sculptures, to the tables-capes for the buffets and the wispy, white-lighted table centerpieces. Twinkle lights abounded and the whole scene was blindly beautiful. It was sensory overload.

More memories from the first night on the show flooded through me: the feeling of being so far out of my league, the insecurity that made me uncomfortable in my own skin, the self-doubt of my appearance. My confidence waned as I stepped off the elevator and into the party.

"You're quiet," Maddox said. His arm was around my waist and he gave me a little squeeze.

"I'm overwhelmed. This is a lot to take in." The room was crowded. Not concert-crowded, but full. Perspiration formed along my hairline and under my arms. It was unnerving. I glanced at Maddox in his tux, looking dapper and debonair and his face calm and relaxed. He was completely in his element. I might've looked the part, standing beside him, holding (really, clutching) onto his arm, but I definitely didn't feel the part.

"Relax, Elsie," he whispered in my ear.

"You can tell I'm nervous?"

"Only because you're gripping my arm so tight it might have to be amputated from the elbow down from lack of circulation."

I loosened my grip. "Sorry."

He guided me through the room to a buffet in the center of the room. "Trust me. You'll do fine. After everyone's had a few drinks, you'll probably feel even more okay."

I wasn't sure if he meant I should have a few drinks, or wait until everyone was a little tipsy so I wouldn't feel so out of place.

"We'll grab some appetizers, mingle a little and soon enough dinner will be served."

Mingling. The word paralyzed me. I didn't want to mingle. What if I was inadequate to make small talk with a bunch of strangers?

"Isn't that the male model who was in the Taylor Swift video?" I asked, zeroing in on a particularly striking guy.

Maddox looked where I gestured. "I think so. At least I think he's a model. I don't know him personally, just met him at a party before."

He said it so casually, like it was no big deal. I didn't want to sit there, awestruck, with my mouth hanging open, so I made a conscious effort to close my mouth. I continued to scan the room, wondering who else I would see. Would I recognize anyone? Would the people be friendly? Was this even going to be a fun party since the only person I knew was Maddox? "How many people do you know at this party? Anyone? Everyone?"

He glanced around. "Yeah, I met some of these people

before. Not exactly friends, just been introduced. My buddies are there," he pointed to a far corner, beyond the wreath ice sculpture in the center, to the windows overlooking the harbor. "We can grab some food at the buffet and head over there. I can finally introduce you to them."

"Great." Anything to be moving, looking like I was engaged in the party, like I belonged at this party, even though I totally didn't feel like I belonged here.

We made our way through the buffet. He chose food that I only partially recognized, such as oysters on the half shell, caviar and some other raw, seafood-looking something. I stuck with foods I could name such as shrimp cocktail, scallops wrapped in bacon, and cubed cheese speared by fancy toothpicks. There were foods named on the buffet that I'd never even heard of.

"This is the fanciest party I've been to, hands down. Including all the weddings I've ever been to, and all the dates and parties I attended on the TV show," I whispered

"Yeah. It's a little over the top. But, it's the Christmas party, so I think they've gone extra-fancy."

"You mean every party you go to isn't always this fancy?"

"No. Some are fancier," he said honestly.

For some reason, that caused a zip of fear to course through me. "Really?"

He shrugged. "Sometimes. But that's more the exception and not the norm."

"That gives me a smidgen of relief." But not enough to quell all of my fears. I reminded myself of my resolve. I could have a good time and enjoy an amazing evening.

I followed his lead, grateful to be holding on to his hand as we weaved our way between tables and across the room. He greeted pretty much everyone we passed, took time to stop and talk with some and introduce me.

"Here's our table," he said as we made it to the front of the room. We took our seat, joining two other couples. "Elsie, Dawson Carter and his girlfriend, Tatiana; his brother, Preston Carter and his date for the evening, Guinevere. This is Brooks Stansfield and his date, Cressida; and the president of 4you2, Ben Harxly and his date Janelly."

We shook hands and made small talk, but I mostly listened. The men started into a lively conversation about something that had happened at work during the week, and I began to heartily eat the food in front of me. It was easier than making small talk.

"I find all that all"—she rolled her eyes—"boring," Tatiana said in a low voice. She was a beautiful girl with golden skin and amber hair.

Surprised that she was directing her comments to me, I swallowed quickly and tried to sound interested. "Really?"

"Yes." She then angled her head and squinted at me closely. "You look so familiar."

"I get that a lot."

"Seriously, I'm sure I've seen you someplace before. Have we met?"

"Do you watch the show *Desperately Seeking Mrs. Right*?"

"I do! I love that show!" She snapped her fingers, her long, sparkly acrylic nails clicking as she did. "That's it. You were on there! What season was that again?"

"Joshua's," I said.

"Yes! Joshua." Her face screwed into a frown. "I was a fan at first, but when it came down to the final three, including you, I stopped liking him. I assume after what he did to you, that you're not a fan, either."

"Nope, not a fan. He was a player and there's a reason why he's still single." Admittedly, that did give me a certain sense of satisfaction. He was a jerk and deserved to be alone until he could figure out how to treat another person, specifically a romantic partner, with respect and honesty. But, now having experienced a taste of having to choose between multiple, great people, I realized why his decision wasn't so clear cut. I still didn't like him, but my criticism had softened a tiny bit.

"He's been on that *Hookup Island* show," said Tatiana

"He does a lot of hooking up but never ends up with anyone." I had enough problems in my own, personal relationships right now to be concerned about Joshua's relationships.

"It's kind of sad, if you ask me," she said.

"I don't know if he's looking for a relationship or just a good time. I think it's the latter. If they keep inviting him, he'll keep going. I'm sure he loves the alcohol and the access to all the girls."

"Have you been invited to be on the island show?"

I nodded and took a sip from my water glass. "Twice. I wasn't interested in being a part of it. Being on *Desperately Seeking Mrs. Right* was enough."

"Even if there are more people to choose from?"

"Yeah. It's brutal on the self-esteem. I decided after the first show I was on that it wasn't for me. I wanted out of the spotlight and out of the competitive dating pool." I had achieved staying out of the spotlight, but not the competitive dating pool.

"Wasn't it so exciting and glamorous being on a TV show? All the parties, the traveling, the evening dresses, relaxing at the pool?"

She named most of the reasons I hated being on the show. Throw a bunch of beautiful, competitive women into a confined space and a lot of alcohol and it was bound to have a bad outcome. "You would think, but no. This is more glamorous than anything I did on the show."

She looked around. "Really?" She drained her glass of the champagne and snagged another one from the waiter passing by.

"Is this the kind of thing you're used to?" I asked.

"We go to a lot of parties. It's fun. We go to Hawaii a lot too. Dawson likes to surf."

I supposed that's what it was like jet-setting the world while dating a young billionaire. Was that what it'd be like if I got into a relationship with Maddox? Time and time again feeling awkward, uncomfortable and out of place? Was it just something that came with the territory of dating him? Or would I eventually get used to it and maybe even bored of it? Would this become the norm?

Tatiana excused herself to get a drink at the bar and the men continued discussing business. I took a moment to study the people seated at the other tables. Everyone in the room seemed cool and collected. I wondered if behind the calm expressions anyone was bored like me.

The conversation Maddox was involved in eventually dwindled as various people came and went.

He took my hand. "Sorry I left you out of the conversation for so long. Business talk. Boring stuff."

It didn't just take business talk to be bored. "I've been amusing myself by people watching. What do you know about them?" I asked Maddox and nodded in the general direction. "The couple with the woman in the blue sequined dress."

"That's Micah and Judith Maxwell. They're married. He's a partner in an investment firm. She's in publishing or something like that."

"What's their backstory? How do you think they met?"

Maddox looked at me, confused. "Why?"

I shrugged. "I don't know. Just making conversation. It's fun to guess backstories."

"I've never played that game," Maddox said. "Seems kind of silly, don't you think?"

There wasn't malice in his voice, but it shut down the fun and curiosity to pursue it. Honestly, I felt a bit chastised. I laced my fingers together and rested them on the edge of the table, forcing myself to maintain a neutral, but interested expression. His friends returned from the bar and they quickly became engrossed in a conversation about business again.

I excused myself and went into the restroom, which also had a sitting room with sofas and mirrors that lined the walls. I sunk into the sofa farthest from the door. With my phone in hand, I pretended to be engrossed in it by scrolling through social media. Really, I wanted to be away from the party scene. I was tempted to unzip my dress just a little, to allow my rib cage to expand to its normal size. The bodice was even tighter now that I'd eaten dinner, but it was the first, and probably only chance, I'd ever had to try Kobe beef and I was not going to pass it up.

"Have you seen Clara Zann?" a chirpy voice said. "She's supposed to be here tonight, but I haven't seen her yet."

I didn't recognize the name, so I continued scrolling through my phone.

"She's probably afraid to show her face." The second girl said before snickering.

I looked up surreptitiously, trying to not be caught eavesdropping, but curious to find out who was speaking. There were two beautiful, waif-like girls standing at a mirror, applying lipstick.

The one who had just spoken had curly hair and wore a

short, black, sleeveless dress that accentuated her thin shoulders.

I didn't recognize either of the girls, but with their looks it was easy to assume they were models or something similar.

Chirpy-voice girl looked around the room, her head stretching to check out who was in the room with them. Her eyes passed over me without an ounce of recognition. "You mean because of her botched plastic surgery?"

Both girls broke out into giggles. It took me a second to realize they had to have at least a few drinks in them.

Curly-hair girl floated her hands over her hair, as if smoothing any strays. "What happened?"

"She was having a lip implant—"

There was such a thing as lip implants? Never heard of that.

"But it's lopsided, or didn't get injected evenly or something like that and now her lips are like this..." Chirpy-Voice screwed her lips into a misshapen expression. "It's like her bottom lip is a fat lip, but only in the corner."

This time the girls laughed uncontrollably. I continued to pretend to be engrossed in my phone, tapping on the screen like I was typing out texts and wasn't aware of their conversation. Of course, with the acrylic nails, I was just tapping and not actually able to do anything.

When they finally caught their breath, Chirpy-Voice wiped her eyes and fixed her smudged eyeliner. "Why is she going to a cheap plastic surgeon anyway? She has enough money to get better results."

Curly-Hair shrugged her bony shoulder, making her collar bone protrude even more. "Dunno. Maybe it was a sale. Or a bundle? Who knows? But her lips look grotesque."

"Guess she'll wear a mask until she gets that fixed." Chirpy-Voice shrieked with laughter

Curly-Hair poked out her lips and pursed them. "She'll end up like this."

They laughed and I wondered how bad this Clara Zann girl's misfortune was. I Googled Clara Zann lip debacle and pictures exploded on my screen, each one worse than the first. It was as bad as they said it was.

Chirpy-Voice grabbed Curly-Hair's arm. "Sssh, ssh, ssh," she said. She put her finger to her lips and both girls lost it again. "She's texting. Ssh!"

Chirpy-Voice scowled at her phone. "We're in the bathroom," she said as she typed.

Curly-Hair stared at her friend's screen. Her hand went to her mouth. "Ooh! She's coming!"

Less than a minute later, a girl I now recognized as Clara Zann entered. "Where have you been? I've been looking all over for you!" She spoke with her hand in front of her mouth.

Chirpy-Voice held up her lipstick. "Touch-ups," she said.

Clara glared at herself in the mirror. "Look at this!" She used all ten fingers to point at her mouth. "It's a disaster! I look like a clown!" she wailed.

"It's not that bad," Curly-Hair said in a soothing voice, wrapping her arms around Clara.

"You can get it fixed, right?" Chirpy-Voice said, with the gentlest of tones.

They were reassuring the girl! Unbelievable! Two minutes before they were making fun of her lips.

Tears gathered in her eyes and she choked on her words. "Yes. Soon. But meanwhile I have to walk around looking like this."

"Are you going back to the same doctor to fix it?" Chirpy-Voice asked.

"No way! What if he messes up as bad as this again? I'm getting a second opinion, getting it fixed and suing the incompetent doctor's butt! No one should have to see this in the mirror."

"You're right. Absolutely! Sue him!" The girls cried in an act of solidarity. "His license should be revoked!"

"What are you looking at?"

Oh, no! I'd been caught. But really, I'd been spacing out. Contemplating how I would survive in a world like this with friends like those. Guessing how much time had passed since we'd arrived and how much longer we'd stay. Wondering what Eric was doing tonight.

"Sorry. Nothing. I'm...looking up how many calories are in a shrimp."

Satisfied, the girls turned their attention back to Clara. "Don't be so hard on yourself. It's really not that noticeable."

"C'mon, let's go. We're missing out on drinks," Chirpy-Voice commanded, looping her arm through Clara's. "I promise, no one will say a thing."

Creating a human wall built by two fake friends and one vulnerable girl, they returned to the party.

Those were not the kind of friends any girl needed. Ever.

I left the bathroom feeling off. Hearing their conversation, watching their interaction, and knowing there were more people like them in the circles Maddox socialized in, I wanted out. Out of the bathroom, out of the party, out of the relationship.

35

"Are you tired?" Maddox asked. We were in his car driving back from the Christmas party, heat blasting, Christmas music streaming. Hidden under my coat, I'd unzipped my dress and was finally able to breathe deep.

"I am."

He reached into his coat pocket and pulled out an envelope. "Here," he said as he handed it to me.

"What's this?" I asked, even though I was pretty sure I already knew. It was the size of a standard Christmas card, but thicker. Maybe he went for the more expensive cards that had lots of layers and details.

"Open it and find out," he said, unable to contain his smile.

I did as I was instructed, and slowly slid my finger under the seal and pulled the card from inside. It wasn't a multi-layered card like I'd assumed. In fact, it was simple: a snowy background with a glittery, decorated Christmas tree as the focal point on thick cardstock. There was definitely something inside. Maybe a gift card.

It wasn't a gift card, or even a pile of cash, but something much simpler: a folded piece of paper. White, plain, folded into fourths. Once unfolded, the simplicity of the gesture opened up to a complex gift.

It was an itinerary.

I turned on my phone flashlight to make sure I was seeing what I thought I saw in the dim lighting of the car.

It was indeed an itinerary.

To Paris.

With him.

For February.

My mouth dropped as my eyes widened. "This is too much," I murmured.

I skimmed over the printing, trying to absorb the details. Paris, France, February. Over Valentine's Day.

"Merry Christmas, Elsie," he said, grinning from ear to ear.

I licked my lips because it felt like my whole mouth went dry, while my heartbeat sped up. "This is my Christmas gift? Um, I don't really know what to say."

"Say yes," Maddox said, his smile now hopeful.

"Uh…" I was still at a loss for words. This gift was huge in so many ways I still couldn't comprehend it at the moment. I had so many questions. Were these non-refundable tickets? What if I couldn't go? What if I could go? This definitely defined our relationship. Or was this like a weekend trip to take and wasn't the big deal I thought it was? So. Many. Questions!

He took my hand and rubbed his thumb over mine. "I hope I wasn't too presumptuous. I know a trip to Europe needs a lot of planning."

And commitment. I didn't want to commit to something I wasn't committed too. But it was Paris! The Louvre! The Eiffel Tower! Baguettes! Pastries!

My pulse raced in my throat and a panicky feeling overtook me.

I was freaking out.

Just a little bit.

I'm allowed to freak out. After all, he just bought me a ticket to Paris.

But a trip to Paris comes with a price.

What exactly would I have to "pay" to go on this trip? Was it the price that bothered me?

I wanted to go to Paris.

But did I want to go with him?

Yes and no.

I liked him.

A lot.

But if I agreed to go on this trip with him, that would mean (at least to me) that I was in an exclusive relationship with him.

The only problem was, tonight at the party, I'd decided to break up with him.

He squeezed my hand. "You don't have to give me an answer right now. Think about it."

I cleared my throat. "I have thought about it. Taking a trip like this, together, is a commitment."

Maddox glanced over at me. "I'm ready to commit," he said, then paused. "But it sounds like you aren't."

That uncomfortable feeling in the pit of my stomach made me feel squirrely. After a deep breath, I answered. "I just can't commit." I shifted my weight trying to get more comfortable, but there was no escaping the feeling. Or the confinement of the car. I should've thought my break up through a little better, or at least picked a better location.

"To who? To me? Or to me *and* the cop?"

Another deep breath. I hated this. I cursed myself for

even getting into this situation. My instinct was to stare at the dashboard, reading every word displayed on the radio. Finally, I forced myself to meet his eyes. "To you."

His chin dropped and his shoulders sagged. Just a little. "Meaning the cop won? Does he know that? Seems strange that you're here with me."

I shook my head. "He doesn't know and I really wasn't trying to make it a competition. I never meant to date two guys. I've tried to follow my heart." I hated the words as they came out of my mouth. Everything I said sounded like it was scripted straight out of *Desperately Seeking Mrs. Right*. But it was all true.

His shoulders drooped even more, if that was even possible.

"You're a great guy, but I don't think I'm the girl for you."

"Or that I'm not the guy for you?" he asked.

I guess that was one way to put it. "I know you'll find a great girl. But I don't feel comfortable in your world."

"Neither did I, at first. It takes a while to feel comfortable in this setting."

"I like you. In fact, I even love you—" Gah! I hated admitting that.

He stared straight ahead, his jaw set. "Then why are you breaking up with me?" He sounded frustrated.

"I care for you. A lot. I want the best for you. I want you to succeed and have the best life that you're working so hard to have. But I love you like a brother."

He pantomimed getting shot in the heart. He gripped his fist against his chest and gasped. "You're killing me, you know that, right?"

My mouth fell open.

"Those are some of the worst words a guy can hear. Brother? Really? It felt like kissing your brother?"

"Well, I've never actually kissed my brother, so I don't know what that feels like. But our kiss didn't do anything for me."

"No fireworks?"

I shook my head.

"No sparks? Embers?"

I shook my head some more. "Sorry."

"Are you sure we don't need to give it more time? Try a little harder? Kiss a little more?"

I chewed on my lip. "No. I really am sorry!"

He rubbed his forehead. "I have failed as a man."

"No, you haven't. You just failed to find the right girl."

"I thought for sure you'd choose me."

Vivian did too. But there wasn't too much more to add to the conversation, so I stared out the window. I had done it. I'd made a decision and I felt the weight of the choice off my shoulders. We drove the rest of the way home in silence, his freaky, quiet car making it worse. The ride felt extra-long and by the time we pulled up to Nana's, I was ready to tuck and roll just to put an end to the evening.

"Thank you," I paused as I gripped the door handle. "For everything."

His eyes met mine. "Is this a final goodbye or a..."

"I'd still like to be friends." Because I did like him as a friend and I had a vested interest in Cowboy.

He pretended he took a shot to the heart. "Uh, you're crushing me. Friend-zoned. That's rough."

"I'm trying to be as gentle as possible."

"Thank you."

"So, um...", there was a long, painful pause. "I'll, um... see you around." Without waiting for his response, I let myself out of the car.

36

I sat in my car, the motor running, outside of Eric's house, feeling like a stalker. It was Christmas Day and I didn't want to interrupt his holiday. Even though it was afternoon, I still worried I'd be intruding. Especially since I wasn't sure it'd be a welcome visit.

Me: Are you home?

The message dots bubbled on my screen.

I held my breath. I wanted him to be home. I wanted to see him again. I missed Eric.

On a whim, I decided to make a peace offering of chocolate chip cookies. I was here to drop them off.

But, at the same time, my heart raced in anticipation. If he was home, then I could see him. We could talk, hopefully, and make things better. Breaking up with Maddox would obviously go a long way in solidifying our relationship, but it could also backfire on me.

McCutey: Yes.
Me: Can I drop something off?
McCutey: Yes.
Me: Right now?

McCutey: OK.

I met him at the front door right as he opened it. Giant barked and slipped out the door before Eric could block him with his leg.

"Giant! Back in! Now!" Eric commanded, pointing inside.

Giant stopped, sniffed my leg and then ran back into the warmth of the house. At least he didn't pee on my foot, because then I'd know I wasn't in good standing with him.

We stayed on the porch and Eric shut the door behind him. "Sorry about that."

I hoped he'd invite me in, but maybe this was better. If things went south, it'd be an easy escape.

I held out a paper plate covered in tinfoil. "Merry Christmas! I made these for you. I miss you and I wanted to say I'm sorry for all I've put you through."

There. I said it. Just blurted it out and now the ball was in his court.

Eric cocked his head as he took the offering. "What about Mr. Billionaire?"

"Well, he bought me a ticket to Paris as a Christmas gift. I can finally go to the Louvre."

He exhaled, creating a white puff of air, and shook his head minutely.

I took it as a sign of resignation.

He ran his hand through his hair. "I can't compete with that, Elsie," he said.

"You don't have to."

"Oh, yeah? Why's that?"

"Because I broke up with him," I said.

"*You* broke up with *him*? Why?"

I met his ocean-blue eyes. "I like you better," I said.

He nodded slowly. "I see. And that's what this is for?" He held up the cookies. "To celebrate?"

"Yes," I said.

He lifted the edge of the foil and sniffed. He blinked a few times and then lifted the rest of the foil. "Did you mean to bring me burned cookies?"

It was true. They were burned. To a crisp. Nana's oven did not register the true temperature, so my cookies were ruined.

"There's a reason I brought them over," I said before making my plea. "I need help. Obviously." I motioned to the cookies and pulled an envelope from my back pocket that held his gift. "I got you this for Christmas," I said and handed it to him.

He opened it, read the card silently, then unfolded the paper. "Cooking classes?"

"I'm hoping you'll not only go with me, but that you'll give me another chance. Otherwise, I'm going to have to take Nana as my date and that's unromantic, embarrassing and not who I want to spend my evening with."

He dropped the plate of cookies, pulled me into his arms and I melted as his lips met mine. I inhaled his scent and relaxed into his embrace, kissing him back. It felt…right.

When we finally broke apart, breathless, he said, "I've missed you too."

EPILOGUE

The February air was cold and a little bit biting as I helped Nana into my car. She insisted I be the one to drive her to her colonoscopy.

It was Valentine's Day, which I thought was a horrible day to schedule such a procedure. Could you even enjoy any chocolate after something like *that*?

"I hope you don't regret asking me to take you." I didn't think I'd be the best post-procedure buddy.

"But you're the one I want by my side," Nana said, laying her hand on my arm.

"Wouldn't my mom be more qualified? Or my dad?"

"My son's grumpy mug would not be the first face I want to see coming out of anesthesia."

"Okay, then, my mom."

"Elsie. You're an adult. You can handle it."

It was one of those adulting things I didn't *want* to handle.

But it was Nana, and I loved her, so I agreed.

"Blast the heat, honey. I've got thin skin," she said.

It just made me sweat under all my layers of clothing.

"Besides, it gives us women a rosy glow to our complexion."

I looked at her, ready to ask her about her odd comment, but she cut me off. "Pay attention to the road, dear. You always seem to get pulled over by the cops when you drive here."

It was true, or had been. Ever since Eric and I had made our relationship official, I was proud to say I'd been a completely law-abiding citizen. I hadn't had any more run-ins with the law except when it was on purpose and with Eric.

Suddenly there was a siren and police lights appeared behind us.

I glanced in my sideview mirror as I guided the car to the shoulder of the road, allowing the police cruiser to pass. It didn't. Instead, it followed me, parking a car length or two behind me. And, from what I could see, the officer wasn't Eric.

"Were you speeding?" Nana asked.

My heart raced as I thought of the last time I glanced at the speedometer. I wasn't speeding. It was my automatic response to the police. That instant thought of *what did I do wrong?*

"I don't think so. I don't know what I did."

I watched the rearview mirror, waiting for the officer to approach.

Did I have another tail light out? My thoughts flashed back to the night when I drove into town and met Eric for the first time.

"You don't have any drugs or guns or anything illegal in here, do you?" Nana asked.

"Nana!" Did she really think I'd have something illegal in my car?

Her comment made me feel panicked. *Calm down, you're being ridiculous.* I hadn't done anything wrong.

"Weird," Nana said, straining to look out the back window. "Another cruiser pulled up."

A loud speaker pierced the air. "Get out of the car with your hands up."

Now I really went into panic mode. "What is going on?"

"It doesn't sound good," Nana said, providing no reassurance at all. "What did you do?"

"I didn't do anything. Why do you think I did something? Maybe they want you," I said, my stress coming through my tone.

"Don't be ridiculous, Elsie. Why would they want me? I haven't been secretly robbing banks while you're working. It is your car. They're pulling *you* over."

Nana's words made me wish I was the one wearing the adult diaper right now instead of her. I did what I was told by the loudspeaker.

That healthy glow Nana had been talking about earlier was now compounded by complete embarrassment, and I was probably beet red. All the layers I had on caused a wave of claustrophobia. I eyed the curb, just in case I needed to sit because I couldn't stand.

The spotlight shined right in my eye when I finally turned and straightened by the car. Why were they using a spotlight? It was barely dusk. The red and blue flashing lights sliced through the last remains of daylight. Even though it was almost dark, I wanted to die. Everyone driving by was sure to be rubbernecking.

And I still had no idea what was going on.

"Ma'am, could I have you stand at the back of the car here, hands on the trunk."

I did as I was told, still stunned that this was happening.

The other officer brought my purse out of the car and placed it in front of me. "Is this your bag?"

"Yes," I said, my words shaky.

He poked around until he produced my wallet. "Is this your wallet?" he asked.

I gulped. "Yes."

He looked inside at my license from arms distance. "Elsie Lawson. Is that you?"

"Yes. And I know Officer McCutty," I stammered, finding my voice.

"Do you now?"

"Yes," I said, gaining some confidence. "I'm his girlfriend."

"His girlfriend? Really? I haven't heard about any girlfriend," the cop said gruffly.

Was he new? Did he work opposite shifts than Eric? Maybe they weren't friends. Maybe Eric didn't talk about me at work or mention anything about a relationship. "If I could call him, I'm sure he could vouch for me and clear this up."

"Do you know what's going on?" the cop asked.

My throat tightened and I blinked back tears. "No, I have no idea."

"Ma'am, we're placing you under arrest. Face forward and put your hands behind your back."

The cold metal cuff snapped on to my left wrist. *What? Why?* I couldn't process what was going on. "I'm under arrest? For what?" Adrenaline pricked at my skin.

"For stealing my heart."

My heart stuttered for a second as I realized that the officer speaking wasn't the first one, but Eric. I turned around, but Eric wasn't standing behind me.

He was down on one knee.

In his hand, he held an open, red velvet box. And inside that box, was an oval diamond ring.

He cleared his throat dramatically. "Elsie Lawson, you have stolen my heart. From that first traffic stop, I feel like fate has brought us together. Will you give up your life of crime and surrender your heart to me? I promise I will love you and care for you for the rest of our lives."

I stood frozen in place, my mouth gaping open.

Time crawled by. Somewhere in the distance I could hear horns honking.

This was really happening.

"Please," he said, pushing the ring closer.

I was finally able to gather my thoughts. "Before I answer, I have one condition," I said.

"Anything," he said, getting to his feet.

"Please uncuff me."

He fumbled for the key. "Of course, sure."

Once freed, I threw myself into his arms and hugged him tightly. "I can't believe you!" I exclaimed. When we pulled apart, I punched him lightly in the shoulder. "You had me totally freaked out. If you ever scare me like that again, I might end up in jail for murder!" I joked, finally feeling the prior rush of adrenaline dissipating.

He held his arms out. "You said you wanted your fiancé to plan something original. This was the best I could do. You know how much permission I had to get from my boss to pull this off?"

I started laughing, finally able to find humor in this situation, appreciating Eric's creativity. I bent over, my hands on my knees, trying to catch my breath.

"You're getting married!" Nana yelled. She gathered us both up into a bear hug. "Welcome to the family, Officer McCutey."

If the Ring Fits

"So, no colonoscopy?" I asked, stepping back to get some air.

Nana dropped her head. "Nope. I made it up. I couldn't think of anything that would get you to go someplace with me at a certain time. This was all about precision timing."

"Thanks, Nana. I couldn't have done it without you," Eric said. "I owe you one."

Snap! Snap! Snap!

Vivian popped up from behind a row of hedges, a DSLR camera hanging from a strap around her neck. "Elsie! Elsie! I'm so excited for you!"

"Where did you come from?" I asked, confused. Had she been here the whole time?

She pointed behind her. "I was taking pictures from over there."

I pictured her like the paparazzi, poking her lense through a gap in the bushes. "You were hiding in the hedge?"

"If you saw me, you'd totally know something was up. So, yeah, I was hiding. This event had to be documented."

I probably could appreciate it more in a couple of hours, once I had come down off the rush of emotions.

I looked from Eric, to Nana and then to Vivian. "You were all in on this?"

"Precision timing," Nana repeated. "Like clockwork."

Eric pointed to the other cops, now smiling. "Don't forget them."

"Congratulations," the officer said and shook our hands. "I'm gonna take off, man," he said to Eric.

"Thanks for helping me out."

"Glad to be a part of this," he said and clapped Eric on the shoulder. He congratulated us one more time before getting back into his cruiser.

I wanted to hug and punch everyone involved. I was so excited and yet was so scared. "Oh, my gosh, you guys! I can't believe you were all in on this."

"You had no idea?" Eric asked.

"No," I said.

He took the ring out of the box and held it out. "You never answered the question. Elsie, will you marry me?"

"Yes," I said.

"Yes?" he repeated, blinking back his happiness.

I nodded fervently. "Yes!"

His arms shot up in the air, in a sign of victory. "Yes! She said yes!"

I held my left hand out so he could slide the ring on my finger.

And I was glad to see, the ring was a perfect fit.

The End

ABOUT THE AUTHOR

Sally Johnson has always had an overactive imagination and writing is how she puts it to good use. To date, she has written nine novels, the latest of which is *If the Broom Fits*. She enjoys watching classic rom-coms, but movies like *Notting Hill, About a Boy,* and *The Wedding Singer* have inspired her quest to explore real life relationships in humorous but grounded fiction.

She is a native of the East Coast, but currently lives on the West Coast in Las Vegas. When not writing, she taxis her kids around, dog-sits, and thrift-shops like a fiend.

For more books and updates, visit *SallyJohnsonWrites.com*

Sally would love to hear from you on social media!

- facebook.com/sallyjohnsonwrites
- instagram.com/sallyjohnsonwrites
- amazon.com/author/Sally-Johnson
- pinterest.com/sallysjb

READ MORE FROM SALLY JOHNSON

The Suddenly Single Series

Suddenly Single (previously published as *The Skeleton in my Closet Wears A Wedding Dress*)

Worth Waiting For (Suddenly Single Series #2)

Anxiously Engaged (coming soon)

The Wit and Whimsy Romance Series

If the Kilt Fits

If the Boot Fits

If the Suit Fits

If the Broom Fits

If the Ring Fits

Standalone Romances

Dear Mr. Darcy

That Thing Formerly Known As My Life

Pretty Much Perfect

Join my newsletter to get all the latest information!

SallyJohnsonWrites.com

Made in the USA
Monee, IL
31 January 2023